AN AVALON CAREER ROMANCE

FOREVER ALOHA
Debby Mayne

Betty Sorenson, sister-in-law of Leilani from *Aloha Reunion*, returns to Hawaii by means of a job transfer. Betty's new boss Mark Diaz is a man who never seems satisfied with anything she does on the job. Since she can't seem to change him, she decides to do a good job and make the most of what she has, even if her boss is a sourpuss.

Mark's goal has never been to climb the corporate ladder, but he feels that he needs to meet his father's expectations. His position in the bank in Hawaii is a compromise—to satisfy his father's ambition for him and to put him close to the waves. He loves surfing, and he does it every chance he gets.

As these two are thrown together, both in and out of the office, she's intrigued by how different he is away from the bank, and she finds herself falling in love with him. He's attracted to everything about her. Is it possible for these two to meet the challenges of their differences and find true love?

FOREVER ALOHA

•

Debby Mayne

AVALON BOOKS
NEW YORK

PRINTED IN THE UNITED STATES OF AMERICA
ON ACID-FREE PAPER
BY HADDON CRAFTSMEN, BLOOMSBURG, PENNSYLVANIA

This book is dedicated to Angela DiMattei and Risa Demers.

Chapter One

This was one of the most significant moments of Betty Sorenson's life. Once she stepped off the plane and placed her foot on Hawaiian soil, she was finally home.

Although she'd spent four years in college on the island of Oahu, and she'd been back several times to visit, for the first time in her life, Betty made the adult decision to choose where she wanted to live. Her decision had nothing to do with where she grew up, her family, or anything else she could put her finger on. This time, she went with what felt right.

"Over here, Betty!" she heard from somewhere off to her right.

By the time she moved toward the familiar voice, she saw her old friend Deanne running up to the gate, the flower leis hanging from her wrist. "Man, this place is crawling with security," Deanne informed her and in the same breath said, "Aloha, Betty. Welcome back."

Betty hugged Deanne before pulling away and looking around. "It's great to be back. Where is everyone?"

"If you're talking about Marlene and Terri, they're both on vacation, visiting friends and family on the mainland. It'll be a while before they're back."

Marlene and Terri were the other two housemates left after Leilani married Betty's brother Jeff and moved into their own place.

"So that means we have the castle to ourselves?"

"Yep," Deanne replied. "Actually, you'll be alone most of the time since I've talked the big boss into double-scheduling me during semester break." She was in graduate school.

"Same boss?"

Deanne's expression became guarded, and she cleared her throat as she quickly turned away. "Uh huh."

Betty made a mental note to ask Deanne about that later. She'd never seen her become flustered, so something else was going on.

On the drive to the "castle," the housemates' affectionate name for the tiny house where four women lived at any given time while in college, Deanne filled Betty in on all the recent events. "You should see Leilani's and Jeff's place," Deanne said as they waited for a light to turn green. "She has that place fixed up like a dollhouse."

"I believe it. Lani's very creative."

Deanne took a deep breath and slowly let it out. "I have a wonderful feeling about you moving back in, Betty. Some wonderful things are going to happen, now that you're back. You bring magic with you everywhere you go."

Betty leaned back, studied Deanne, then laughed out loud. "I don't have any magical powers, so I don't know why you'd say that."

"Oh, but you do. You're the most magical person I've ever met. Things always happen when you're around."

The two of them exchanged a smile, then rode in comfortable silence the rest of the way. Betty loved the fact that she knew Deanne well enough to not have to keep the conversation running constantly.

As always, the house appeared to be sitting there, welcoming, when they pulled into the gravel drive-way. While the world around them changed as fast as the days went by, this house remained the same.

"Maybe I should make an offer to buy the castle," Betty said as she got out. "When we outgrow it, I can rent it to younger coeds."

"Not a bad idea. Let's get your stuff inside. We'll talk about that later."

It took them several trips before all of her luggage was inside. She'd be sharing Deanne's room as she settled in her new job at the bank. To her surprise, the transfer to Hawaii came along with a promotion and a much higher salary. The man who once held her new job had taken a surprise early retirement.

"I still can't believe this is happening," Deanne said. "One day you're talking about the possibility of moving back, and the next day you're here." She snapped her fingers. "Just like that."

"It wasn't that easy."

"Well, it certainly seemed that way."

Without having to be invited, Betty went to the refrigerator to help herself to a snack. They'd always had an unwritten rule that unless there was a note on the food, it was available to anyone who wanted it.

"Mmm, sushi. Is it fresh?"

"Leilani had it sent over this morning for your homecoming. She said it's your favorite kind."

Leilani's uncle had a Hawaiian deli, and she often came in with her arms loaded with various types of sushi. Betty helped herself to a plate filled with rice and seaweed cakes with a little soy sauce on the side.

"Seeing anyone special lately?" Betty didn't look up, instead focusing on her plate. She reached down and lifted one slice of sushi to her mouth, savoring the taste she'd missed since leaving. Arizona had sushi bars, but they weren't the same.

Deanne's silence caused Betty to stop eating and look up. There was definitely something going on with her, but Deanne wasn't ready to talk about it.

"Okay," Betty finally said, "so there's a mystery man in your life you don't want to talk about. Tell me when you're ready, okay?"

With a half-smile, Deanne lifted one shoulder. "It's not that I don't want to talk about him, it's just that I'm afraid I might jinx something and I'll be right back to where I was before."

"That's silly. But if you believe that stuff, I understand."

"When do you start your new position?"

"Next week."

"At least you get a break."

"Not much of one. I have to do some serious shopping. I don't have much to wear to work."

"What did you wear in Arizona?"

"Mostly business suits."

"Women wear suits here."

With a nod, Betty said, "Yeah, but these are wool. I need some summer suits and brighter colors. I don't want to be known as 'Betty the Drab One.' "

Deanne laughed out loud. "I don't think anyone will ever accuse you of that. You're the least drab person I know."

Betty was well aware that her friends thought she was smart, confident, and some had even called her effervescent. However, she had plenty of doubts, and she often wondered how she'd fooled so many people.

After her snack, Betty pushed away from the table. "I think I'll go rest for a while. I'm wiped out."

"Good idea. I have to go pick up my paycheck, then I have a few errands to run. My cell phone number's on the bulletin board by the kitchen phone."

Betty was glad to be alone for a little while, so she

could absorb the sounds and smells of this fabulous island. She'd missed it so much she ached, and now she was back for good—at least for as long as she could see into the future. Of course, things could happen, and she could find herself facing something unexpected that would drive her back to the mainland. Hopefully, that wouldn't happen any time soon.

The week went by rather quickly, since she caught up on her sleep and shopping. By the time Betty started her new job, she had a new suit for every day of the week as well as a refreshed mind and attitude. She was ready to go to work.

"Great to have you, Betty," Andrea, the local human resources director told her. "I'm just glad we don't have to teach you the customs of Hawaii. It's about time they promoted someone who knew their way around Hawaii."

With a practiced smile, Betty nodded. "I'm happy to be here. I really missed everything about this place."

They chatted for a few minutes, until the phone rang. "Oh, good," Betty heard Andrea say into the phone, "she's right here. I'll send her down." Once she was off the phone, she glanced up at Betty and smiled. "They're ready for you in operations. Call my extension if you need anything, okay?"

Betty took the card she was offered and nodded. Her heartbeat accelerated as she got closer to the elevator, but she kept her composure until the doors closed and she punched the floor button. Once no one could see her, she dropped the smile and took a deep breath. She was scared out of her mind. When she'd first started at the bank in Arizona, no one had any expectations of her because she went right into a management training program, fresh out of college. She'd worked her way into various positions, most of them newly created, and she'd been able to define her jobs, practically writing her own job descriptions. But now, she was stepping into the shoes of someone who'd recently retired—or at least that's what she understood the situation to be. The director of human resources for this region had been sort of vague. She figured she'd find out what the deal was once she got into her new position. And now here she was.

The doors opened, and she plastered that smile of confidence right back on her face. A man greeted her in the lobby, his hand extended.

"I'm Mark Diaz, internal auditor and director of operations for all of Hawaii," he said.

Betty offered a crisp, businesslike nod. "Nice to meet you, Mr. Diaz."

"I'll be going over the books with you from day one." He'd started walking toward the hall, so Betty followed—at least that's what she assumed she was supposed to do.

"Is your office in this branch?" she asked.

He chuckled. "I have an office in every branch. And you never know when I might pop in and use it."

Betty grimaced. His initial friendliness had quickly been taken over by what sounded an awful lot like cynicism. That disturbed her. Couldn't he at least give her a short honeymoon in her new position?

"Here's your office," Mr. Diaz said as he gestured toward a small room with a door that was partially propped open. "I hope you don't mind that I switched when Dunstan got canned."

Betty whipped her head around to face him. "Dunstan got canned? I thought he retired."

Another chuckle that sent her nerves to the edge of her skin. "Retired?" An uncomfortable pause fueled her jitters. "I guess that might be one way of looking at it. He'd been with the bank about twenty years, and he had a little money in his retirement account. He's lucky we let him keep it."

The office was small and bare, but it was nicely appointed. As Betty looked around, she saw that the only furniture was a large mahogany desk, a leather chair, and a sleek looking file cabinet that matched. But it had a view.

"You can see the city from here," Mark informed her. "I hope you're comfortable."

"Oh, I'm sure I will be," Betty said. "Now I need to get some papers and a computer in here, and it'll feel like an office."

He held her gaze for a moment then glanced away. "The books are being audited, so it'll be a few days before we set you up. In the meantime, I thought we'd put you through an informal orientation."

"Orientation?" Betty had been through the corporate three-day orientation when she'd first started.

He nodded. "We don't exactly do things the same way here."

"More casual?"

Mr. Diaz sniffed and took a step away from her, but he didn't meet her gaze this time. "No, quite the contrary, Ms. Sorenson. We run a tight ship around here, and I won't tolerate anything less."

Betty felt her childhood insecurities rise to the surface, but she took a deep breath and made a fist that she hid behind her back. She'd been brought up with an over-achieving brother who was the town sweetheart, and she always had a lot to live up to. Now she had to prove herself to this tyrant of a boss who seemed bent on not trusting her. Whatever Harry Dunstan had done must have been a humdinger.

He shifted his weight from one foot to the other, catching her attention and causing her to look directly at him. "But I'm sure you're up to it, or you never would have gotten this job. You came with some high recommendations."

"I've always done a good job, er . . . Mr. Diaz. And I plan to continue to do this." In the past, Betty had been on a first-name basis with coworkers, regardless of their level in the company. Until Mark Diaz told her otherwise, she'd call him Mr. Diaz.

"Good. Now let's go into my office so we can go over your new job description."

Betty had held a half dozen positions with First Guardian Bank, but she'd never encountered anyone like Mark Diaz, whose power seemed to have gone to his head. She let out a deep sigh. Oh well, at least she had a pleasant place to go to each night, where she could let her hair down among longtime friends.

As Mr. Diaz went on and on about his expectations, she only half listened. He wasn't bad looking when he dropped the scowl that had replaced the smile thirty seconds after she'd met him. His smile was quite nice. Warm, even. Although she couldn't be sure, she thought his shoulders might be broad, and his waist small for someone of his height, which she thought to be six-foot-something. It was hard to tell, now that they were sitting down.

"Ms. Sorenson?" He rapped a pencil so hard on the desk, she jumped.

"Uh, yes, Mr. Diaz?"

"Have you ever worked this system before? I know you were director of operations at your old branch, but I understand each region uses different software."

"Uh, yes, I think I'm somewhat familiar with this system." She really needed to pay better attention to what he was saying and less to what the man looked like.

He leaned toward her and squinted. "I want you to know this system inside and out. It's very important in your position."

"Yes, sir," she said crisply. If he wanted to sound like a drill sergeant, she'd treat him like one.

To Betty's surprise, he leaned back, twirled the pencil between his fingers, and shook his head as he laughed softly. "I'm sorry, Ms. Sorenson, if I'm coming across as the gestapo. It's just that after what happened with Dunstan, I'm pretty reactive."

Was he going to tell her, or did she have to ask? This man wasn't exactly the most approachable man she'd been around, so she still wasn't sure what she should do.

"You don't know what happened, do you?" he said, still leaning away from her.

Betty slowly shook her head. "No, I wasn't told. It was my understanding that his retirement was voluntary due to many years of service."

He pondered her response, then said, "Don't ask, okay?" Well, that answered that. She'd have to find out through the grapevine, which might take a while, considering how stuffy this place seemed once she got outside human resources. For a bank in Hawaii, it sure was awfully stiff, completely unlike all the other businesses around here—at least that she was aware of.

The day seemed to drag, but finally, Mr. Diaz, or Mark, whichever one she should call him—she wasn't sure yet—told her she'd done enough for one day. Betty had admitted that she'd never seen some of the methods. "I know this is all new to you, but my system isn't hard. It's just very thorough."

Betty smiled back at him as she thought, *his system? What about the bank's system?* But she didn't say a word. She just kept smiling and grinding her teeth.

The outside air was fresh and sweet smelling, in contrast to the inside of the bank. Betty glanced around at all the flowered dresses and shirts and let out a much needed sigh of relief. This was, indeed, paradise—if only she could get past her new job and not worry. Given her new boss, that might be tough.

Betty didn't have a car yet, so she took the city bus. Nothing had changed, the bus stops were still the same.

As she walked through the door to the castle, Deanne smiled up at her from the floor in front of the stereo, where it appeared she was organizing the CDs and incorporating Betty's into their collection. "Hey, how'd the first day go?"

"Grr. Don't ask." Betty took off her new lime-green jacket and draped it over the back of the sofa and at the same time kicked off her shoes, wiggling her toes. "Ahh. Freedom," she said as she sank down beside her jacket, flopped back and closed her eyes.

"That bad, huh?" Deanne never dropped her dazzling smile, which never failed to light up a room. "What happened?"

"Are you sure you wanna know?"

"Oh, yeah, but just a minute. I need to get something to drink. Want some juice?" She stood up and tugged at the frayed bottom of her cutoffs as she headed toward the kitchen.

"Sure, sounds good."

Deanne left and came back minutes later with two glasses of pineapple juice. Betty took a sip and smiled.

"Well? Are you still glad you're here?" Deanne asked as she sat back down on the floor, cross-legged. "Any regrets yet?"

"No, no regrets," Betty replied. She struggled to come up with the correct response of what she was feeling now. Granted, her new job seemed more like work than her previous position back in Arizona, but she was still glad to be here. "Just a few concerns, that's all."

"Want to talk about it?"

With a shrug, Betty lifted her feet to the coffee table. "Maybe later, once I get things straight in my mind. Today was overwhelming, and I don't even know where to begin."

Deanne turned back to her CDs. Silence fell over the room while she moved them around in the display case. It took her another half hour before they were all organized and put away.

"There," she said. "All set. Just like you never left."

"What're you doing for dinner tonight?" Betty asked.

"Want pizza?"

"Sounds good. Nick's still deliver?" Deanne's shy glance away captured Betty's attention. "What?"

"Steve's picking one up and bringing it to us."

"Steve? Your boss?"

"Yeah. He's coming over for dinner. I hope you don't mind." Although Deanne didn't look her in the eye, Betty had a much better idea of what was going on.

"So you finally agreed to go out with him, huh?"

"Well, yeah, but we're still just friends."

Friends my foot. Betty couldn't help but smile back. "That's the best way to start out in a relationship."

For the first time Betty could remember since Deanne's heart was broken by Jeff, Deanne wasn't smiling. Her expression was serious and tense.

"Look, Betty, this isn't what I'd call a relationship yet. I'm taking things nice and slow."

"That's a good idea." Considering Deanne's track record with men, she meant it, too.

"I like Steve. Always have. It's just that . . ." Her voice trailed off, but Betty didn't push for more. She thought she understood.

"Steve's a nice guy," Betty offered when it was obvious that Deanne wasn't going to finish her sentence. "And a pretty good businessman, too."

Deanne's smile returned, and the whole room seemed brighter. "If you met him on the street, you'd never know the man owned a dozen surfboard rental stands and shops, and a bunch of malasada and manapua wagons all over the islands."

Betty agreed. "I always thought he had the tourist market figured out to a T. The man's brilliant."

Still beaming, Deanne agreed. "Yes, I think so."

Okay, so that explained Deanne's pensive mood. Betty had been fairly certain a man was responsible for the mood she'd found Deanne in when she first stepped off the plane, but until now she didn't realize how significantly.

Deanne was known for having a new guy in her life every couple of months. Right when things would start heating up with any degree of seriousness, she moved on and broke hearts—with the exception of the relationship with Jeff, who'd done the heart breaking. But Deanne had rebounded quickly and become friends with Jeff, almost as if she'd never expressed her undying love for him. Betty had been relieved since Jeff was her brother, and her first allegiance was to her family.

"Let me go change before Steve gets here," Betty said standing up.

She went back to her bedroom and put on some shorts and a tank top. When she returned, the pizza had arrived, and the man she hadn't seen in years was standing in the kitchen looking down adoringly at Deanne. He was in love, Betty could tell.

"Hiya, Steve."

"Aloha. Great to see you again, Betty," Steve said as he crossed the room and offered her an easy hug.

"What kind did you get?" Betty peered down into the pizza box to redirect her attention. She didn't want to make Deanne uncomfortable with her stares, but she was pretty amazed at the fact that these two people had actually gotten together. It wasn't as if Steve hadn't tried off and on over the years. It was more that Deanne literally shrugged him off, saying he wasn't fun enough or that he was too businesslike for her. Apparently, one or both of them had changed.

"How's the new job?" Steve asked as they settled down at the table with their plates.

"It'll take some adjusting." Betty glanced over at

Deanne, who winked and smiled before taking another bite of pizza.

"I know some of the people at First Guardian," Steve said. "My first business loan came from them."

"Oh, really?" Betty hadn't thought about Steve needing a business loan for what he did, but why not? Even though it seemed like just a little haphazardly put-together surfboard stand, she knew it was a thriving business. "Do you by any chance know Mark Diaz?" Her new boss's name caught on her tongue.

Steve beamed up at her. "Yeah, I know da guy. He's one of my best customers."

Both Betty and Deanne nearly choked on their pizza. "You're kidding, right?"

Chapter Two

Betty couldn't imagine the stuffed-shirt Mark Diaz negotiating the waves on a surfboard. She finished chewing her pizza, and stared at Steve, waiting for him to tell her more.

"Yeah, when the bigwigs come from the mainland, he likes to enroll them in a couple of surfing lessons," Steve replied. "It's pretty funny, really."

"I bet it is," Betty replied as a very unlikely visual image of her boss faded from her mind.

Deanne scrunched her nose. "Are you two talking about that Diaz guy who gives the hundred-dollar tips?" She looked to Steve, who nodded, then she turned to Betty. "That guy's totally hot."

Hot? Mark Diaz? Surely, they must be talking about different men. Sure, he looked very handsome in the suit, before he started scowling.

Steve laughed. "Maybe you better not be talking about Betty's boss that way. I wouldn't want him to lose credibility by being 'hot.' "

Deanne stuck her tongue out at Steve then turned to Betty. "Really, Betty, you should see him surf."

"He rents boards from you?"

"No," Deanne said, shaking her head. "He has his own boards. He doesn't even hang out at my stand. Last week, when Steve and I went up to the North Shore, we saw him. That man's good."

Betty shook her head. Do wonders never cease? Imagine, Mark Diaz surfing the waves and letting something else be in control. That was something she couldn't picture.

Deanne changed the subject as they finished their pizza. Steve stood up to help clear the table. "Deanne and I are going to a movie. Wanna go?"

"No, I don't think so," Betty said. "Not tonight. I have a gazillion things to do. The two of you go ahead and have a good time."

It took the three of them less than five minutes to clean the kitchen. After Deanne and Steve were gone, Betty sat back down at the table and buried her face in her arms she'd folded over the table. Everything and everyone were so intertwined, the events seemed almost planned. Of course, Oahu wasn't a very big island, but what were the odds of Deanne actually knowing Mark Diaz?

She got ready for bed early and slid under the soft sheets. Her day had taken so much emotional and mental energy, Betty was exhausted. She picked up the novel she'd started on the plane and read a few pages before her eyes grew heavy and she gave in to sleep.

Mark wasn't sure he was up to training another new person on his system—not this soon after the last couple of fiascoes. After he'd had to testify against Harry Dunstan in the internal audit, he'd moved on to train a new operations manager on the Big Island. Why this particular person had been put into this demanding position, he'd never understand. It had taken him nearly a month to explain the basics, and he still had to field phone calls from the woman who still hadn't gotten it.

"It's so complex," she'd said.

"Well, Nancy, one of these days, it'll just click."

"I certainly hope so," she squeaked, her voice being the proverbial nails on the chalkboard.

Good thing Nancy was in charge of the operations of the smallest branch of First Guardian Bank of Hawaii. What worried him was his pride and joy, the Honolulu Downtown branch, the one that was now in the hands of Betty Sorenson.

When the higher-ups had contacted Mark and asked him to devise a new operations system and test pilot it in Hawaii, he'd been thrilled at the opportunity to show what he was capable of. However, it hadn't taken Harry Dunstan long to figure out a way to cheat the system. Fortunately, Mark had some built-in protection that would not only stop anyone from unscrupulous behavior, it caught him in the act, making the process of getting rid of the crook much easier. The management of the bank knew something wasn't right with Dunstan, and now they knew precisely what he'd been doing, thanks to Mark's system.

Mark had volunteered to act as operations manager of the biggest branch in Hawaii until he had time to find the best replacement for Dunstan. He fully expected them to take him up on his offer, until he'd gotten that phone call a month ago, telling him he'd be training someone who'd been with the bank for a couple years and that she was coming over from the mainland. He started to argue, but stopped to keep from sounding uncooperative. Mark knew this bank operated under a team-based management style, and he didn't want to rock any boats. But still . . .

Being the only child of a successful corporate executive, Mark always felt he had a lot to live up to in his parents' eyes. The brief time he'd lived in Hawaii, Mark had taken up surfing, something his father thought was a waste of time.

"Why can't you play more competitive sports, like football or baseball?" his father had asked. "Surfing won't prepare you for the hard, cold realities of this competitive business world."

Although Mark loved all sports, he especially enjoyed surfing. It gave him a sense of freedom and oneness with nature. His own power paled compared to that of the ocean, and he felt an incredible sense of accomplishment when he could ride the wave all the way to the shore. He suspected it was the same feeling a rodeo rider got when he made it to the end of the show.

As a teenager, Mark never thought it was possible that his father could add more pressure than he already had. But when Mark finished his college degree in business, the push really began. All his father could talk about was "making it to the top." Granted, Mark wanted to be successful, but making it to where his father was didn't seem all that attractive.

Mark interviewed with several companies on the mainland, but when the position of junior auditor of First Guardian Bank was offered in Hawaii, he jumped at it. At first, his father thought it was a silly, impulsive move, but when Mark explained that the chief auditor was nearing retirement, things changed. Mark currently held the highest position he could in his field, without having to move back to the mainland. And now, his father was starting to work on him again to keep moving upward.

"Don't box yourself in, son," he'd told Mark.

Mark was perfectly happy in his job—at least until that new woman, Betty Sorenson, arrived. He'd have to keep a close eye on her. He couldn't afford another scandal, even if he was on the righteous side. Mark wanted to keep a low profile and do a good job without incident.

Sleep came easy to Mark, as it always did. He worked out everyday, and he kept his business clean at the office. There was never any reason to worry, even when he was annoyed.

The next morning, Mark arrived at the office an hour early. He wanted to get a head start so Ms. Sorenson would have her computer as soon as possible. Hopefully, she wouldn't be as dense as Nancy on the Big Island, but he didn't want to count on anything. If he needed to spend more time with Ms. Sorenson, he would. That was part of his job. The only problem was that it meant more time at the office, and he was eager to try out his new surfboard.

Andrea from human resources had nothing but good things to say about Betty, but as far as he was concerned, the jury was still out on her. She seemed to catch on fairly quickly so far, but they'd merely scratched the surface of what all he needed to teach her.

Mark never thought of his system as being particularly difficult, but others had expressed frustration until they got past the learning curve. Hopefully, that wouldn't take too long for Betty.

By the time Mark reached his office, he'd worked himself into a mental stew over all the extra work training Betty Sorenson would surely create. He booted up his computer and clicked on the program that brought him to his ever-evolving training program. Then he clicked on "Print" and looked up just in time to see Betty standing in his doorway.

"Mr. Diaz?" she said, her eyebrows raised, a tentative smile on her lips.

As his eyes grazed her from head to toe, Mark realized how professional yet attractive she looked. She wore a navy colored, short sleeved jacket, with a knee-length skirt to match. Her floral print shirt softened the look of the suit, giving her a feminine edge. He looked back at her face, which had very little makeup, highlighting her best features—her high cheekbones and her soft lips. Mark licked his own lips, then coughed. She tilted her head to one side and looked at him questioningly.

"What do you want me to do first?" she finally asked, breaking the silence.

Mark reached down and picked up the page that had just come out of the printer. "Take this and look it over. I'll answer any questions you have, then we'll go from there."

Rather than leave with the paper, Ms. Sorenson stood in his office and read it, her eyes traveling fast down the page. Twice. She nodded.

"Questions?" he asked, folding his hands in front of him.

Shaking her head, she replied, "No, not really. This is all pretty much common sense."

He'd thought so, too, until several people already in her position had pumped him with questions about his system. Maybe she was just trying to make a good impression on him.

Gesturing toward the chair on the other side of the desk, Mark said, "Have a seat. Let's go over it."

"Okay." She carefully sat down, tugging her skirt

to her knees, which were hard for him not to study. This woman had very shapely legs, athletic yet not too muscular.

"Why don't we start by you explaining the system to me as you understand it." he began.

Leaning forward, taking one more quick glance at the paper in her hands, Betty started talking. She started at the logical spot, the beginning, and worked her way down from there. She summarized his program in a way that truly impressed Mark.

"Very good," he said. "I'm impressed." And he was. The problem was, he wasn't sure what to do next. With everyone else, the first part took several days. Betty took—Mark glanced at his watch—twelve minutes. Wow!

"Would you like me to work on some bank records and show you how well I understand it?" she asked.

"Uh, no, not yet." Call him a control freak or a power pig. Just don't call him careless. After his experience with Dunstan, Mark wasn't about to let her loose with his bank's records—at least not until she passed the next phase.

Holding her hands out to her side, she shrugged. "Then what?"

"Let me pull up the next page. You can go back to your office and work on it until lunch, then we can discuss it this afternoon."

"Okay, fine," she said.

The woman was very agreeable, but he could see her irritation. Mark was well aware of her previous position and how much responsibility she had, but her background was similar to Dunstan's early career. He had to be thoroughly convinced she was honest and understood what she was doing.

The only sound in the room was the printer as it cranked out Betty's next "lesson," which Mark hoped would take her a little more time than the first one. Sure, he knew he was contradicting himself, but at this rate, she'd be actively doing her job by the end of the first week, something he was nowhere near prepared for.

Betty took the sheet without waiting for him to hand it to her. She glanced at it and then nodded as she walked out the door. He thought she'd gone when she backed up and stuck her head back in. "I'll have all this memorized by lunch, and we can move on to the next lesson, Mr. Diaz."

Once she was gone, Mark rubbed his eyes. He'd hoped she had a good enough head on her shoulders to grasp his concepts, but he hadn't counted on this. Was it too much to ask for him to want normal people—and not the extremes?

All morning, Mark tried hard to do all his regular business so he could focus on Betty in the afternoon. But his mind was restless and her image kept appearing every time he shut his eyes.

The phone rang and Mark jumped. "Hello, Mark Diaz here." His voice came out more of a growl than a greeting, and he tried to force himself to relax.

"Uh, Mr. Diaz, I was wondering what time you wanted to go over this second lesson."

"Whenever you're ready, Ms. Sorenson."

"I'm ready now."

He coughed to keep himself from growling again. "Okay, then come on back in here . . . Wait, on second thought, let me come to your office, okay?"

"Are you sure? I can come there."

"No, that's okay. We can meet in your office this time."

After Mark hung up, he thought about the reason he wanted to go to Betty rather than having her come to him. After she'd left his office earlier, her scent had lingered, and it had taken a very long time for him to concentrate. In fact, he still wasn't sure it was gone. Inhaling deeply, then slowly letting out his breath, he realized that whatever fragrance she'd been wearing had evaporated. To his surprise, he was filled with disappointment.

Mark had been in Betty's office less than ten minutes before he realized she was ready for the third part of his training. What was this woman doing to him?

When Betty began looking at her watch every few minutes, Mark realized he was starting to get hungry. "Got plans for lunch?" he asked before he realized what he was doing.

"Well, yeah," she said with some hesitation.

Good. He had no intention of having lunch with her,

anyway. "Then meet me back here in one hour. I don't believe in long lunch hours."

"Yes, sir," she said. "Can you give me the next print-out, just in case I come back early? I don't want to waste any more time on this than necessary."

Waste time? She thought she was wasting time? Mark had to bite the inside of his cheek to keep from letting her know he'd spent weeks on this program, fine-tuning it and making it clear and concise. This was not wasting time.

Betty hurried from the office building as fast as her pumps would carry her. As she rushed over to the travel agent three doors down, she pulled out her cell phone and punched in the number of the castle. Deanne answered on the first ring.

"Well? How's the second day of work?"

Betty shuddered. "You don't want to ask. My boss is the most uptight man I've ever met in my life. He has a system designed to teach morons how to do my job."

"Did you tell him that?" Deanne asked with a giggle.

"Oh yeah, like I'm sure that would go over big."

"I guess it wouldn't be a good idea," Deanne said. "But maybe you should say something."

"No, I think I'll let him go through his entire training program. I'll be the good little monkey he wants me to be, then he won't be able to complain to the regional manager about me."

"Good plan. That's why you're where you are, and I'm in graduate school, trying to be the best geek I can. In my field, we're allowed to tell people what we really think. The bosses just call that eccentric."

"I'd like to be eccentric right now," Betty said as she entered the travel agency office. "But I have to get plane tickets for my parents. The reason I called you is to find out when Jeff and Lani will be back."

"Um, I'm not sure," Deanne said. "Jeff had some business in Japan, and Lani wanted to do a little sight-seeing while they were there."

"Must be nice."

"Yeah, that's what I say."

"Do you think it'll be safe to get the tickets for next month?"

"Should be okay in a month."

"Good, then that's what I'll do." Betty said good-bye, then clicked the phone shut.

While she was at the agency, she managed to get the plane tickets from Arizona as well as a room over-looking the ocean in the Outrigger Hotel. Her parents would be thrilled. They'd stayed there before, and they loved the location and ease of getting around from their "spot" on the beach.

On the way back to the office, she grabbed a ham-burger to go and carried it back with her. Hopefully, Mr. Diaz wouldn't disturb her while she took a much needed break.

No such luck. He was at her door within seconds

of when she'd sat down and unwrapped her hamburger.

"That was quick," he said as he leaned against the door frame, his arms folded over his chest.

The strain of his jacket over his broad expanse of shoulders caught Betty's eye. She had to force herself to look nowhere on Mark but his face, or she feared she might show too much of what she was thinking.

"I hurried through my errand and grabbed this so I wouldn't be late," she said. So far, she'd only taken one bite, and her hunger had faded. She laid the sandwich down.

"Don't let me interrupt your lunch, Ms. Sorenson," he said as he pulled away from the door. "Go ahead and finish. We have work to do this afternoon, and I don't want to be the cause of an eating disorder." He left as quickly as he'd arrived.

Betty wanted to let him know that she'd never had an eating disorder in her life, and she never intended to have one. She wasn't one of those emotional women who held back eating when they had issues. After a brief glance down at her uneaten hamburger, Betty slowly pushed it away. She simply wasn't hungry anymore, that's all.

Chapter Three

Betty wanted to throw herself in a volcano for being so attracted to Mark. No, she wanted to go find the nearest shrink and find out if some wires had come loose in her brain.

What was she thinking?

Okay, calm down. This is an emotional time in a woman's life—changing jobs at the same time as moving across the Pacific Ocean. Any woman would have the same problem.

But Betty wasn't just any woman. She was the one who always remained in control. The smart one. The one everyone else came to for advice.

She leaned back in her leather chair, closed her eyes, inhaled and slowly counted to ten. As she allowed her lungs to release the air, a sound at the door grabbed her attention.

"Uh, Ms. Sorenson," the familiar male voice said, "I almost forgot. We have a staff meeting at three." Mr. Diaz's eyes strayed from her face down to where her hands gripped the desk.

"Staff meeting?" Betty glanced down at her hands and saw that she was white-knuckled, she was holding on so tight. She quickly let go and had to catch herself to keep from falling backward.

The corners of his lips turned up, but he didn't smile. Somehow, he managed to turn what started as a pleasant expression to a dour look, as if he was afraid she might catch him having fun.

"Here's the rest of your training material," he said as he dropped the papers on her desk. "I thought it over and figured you could go at your own pace."

"Thanks, Mr. Diaz."

He narrowed his eyes, crisply nodded, and turned away. "I'll see you at three." Then he paused and added, "No, make that five till three."

"Five till?"

"Yes. I don't want to risk having us walk in after everyone else is seated."

"Oh, I see," she said. "That's fine. Five till."

After he was gone, this time Betty was much more careful. She now realized he was likely to return unexpectedly.

Betty picked up the papers and thumbed through them. He sure spent a lot of time putting this stuff together. Most of it was either common sense or information she'd learned in her initial management training program. Why did Mr. Diaz feel the need to revise it for the Hawaii branches?

This time when the knock came at the door, she expected her boss, but it was a petite woman with big brown eyes and dark blond hair. "Ms. Sorenson?"

"Yes?"

"I wanted to stop by and welcome you. I'm Fran, your secretary."

Betty stood and walked around from behind her desk, her hand extended. "Fran, it's so nice to meet you. I didn't realize I had a secretary."

The woman offered a nervous laugh. "They didn't tell you?"

"No, but I'm very happy to know you're here. How long have you worked for First Guardian?"

Fran frowned as her eyes rolled upward. "Let's see," she said, putting her finger on her chin. "Two years, three months, and four days."

"Wow, you must keep track of every day you're here."

"I'm into statistics and details," Fran said with a matter-of-fact nod. "That's why Mr. Dunstan hired me."

"Mr. Dunstan hired you?" Betty asked, surprised.

"Well, he didn't technically hire me, but he's the one I had my final interview with. If you'll keep a secret, I'll tell you something I never could say to him."

"Sure, Fran," Betty said, now amused at her new secretary. "What's that?"

"He was long overdue for retirement. He was starting to do some really odd things around here."

Betty was dying to ask questions, but she noticed that Mr. Diaz was lingering in the hall a few doors down, and she wasn't sure if he could hear their conversation. Her questions would have to wait.

"Hopefully, I'll learn my job quickly, and we can get down to business soon."

"Oh, I'm sure," Fran said. "I've heard nothing but glowing reports about you."

"That's good."

"Yes, in fact, I even called your secretary back in Arizona, and she said you were very good to her."

Betty loved her staff back in Arizona, and she felt a quick tug of homesickness. But that was silly. She'd wanted to come to Hawaii so much, she was willing to leave everything and everyone behind.

"I'm sure we'll have an equally rewarding relationship, Fran," Betty told her new secretary. "Let me know if there's something pressing, but in the meantime, I really need to get back to studying. Mr. Diaz wants me to learn all that stuff as quickly as possible." She gestured to the stack of papers on her desk.

"Oh, I overheard him telling someone in human resources it'll take you months to learn your job."

Betty grinned on the outside but inwardly seethed. This Fran woman sure was a talker. She'd have to remember to keep her secrets to herself around her. "I'm trying to go a little faster than that."

"No doubt you will," Fran said as she backed away from the door.

Betty pushed her hair back from her face. She'd been blessed with hair that behaved, even in the humid, warm climate of Hawaii. As long as she kept her light brown-streaked-with-honey colored hair cut shoulder length, there was just enough wave to give it body but not enough to make it frizzy.

Now that she knew what Mark Diaz expected from her, she'd be able to set a goal and prove him wrong. Months? If humanly possible, Betty planned to know everything she needed to know by the end of her second week. Everything she'd ever set out to do, she almost always did—with the exception of beating her brother Jeff in a foot race.

That afternoon, when she got home, Deanne and Steve were outside waxing surfboards. "What's going on here?" she asked as she came up the sidewalk from the bus stop. She'd decided to wait a few days before shopping for a car.

"I'm selling some old boards so I can replace them with new stock for rental," Steve said. "We're making them pretty and shiny. Care to buy one?"

Betty lifted one eyebrow. "You're kidding, right?"

"Your brother's a good surfer. I figured it must run in the family."

"Sorry to disappoint you, Steve, but you won't catch this girl on a surfboard in this lifetime."

"Aw, I bet you'd be good."

With a chuckle, Betty headed up the front porch steps. She was exhausted, and all she wanted to do was what she did everyday after work—change into something comfortable and relax.

Deanne followed her inside. "I'll get you something to drink, then you can join us."

"Have you had dinner yet?" Betty asked. "Or are you and Steve going somewhere?"

"Steve has to leave in a little while. He has a few business deals to take care of. Why don't we go for a walk and grab something while we're out?"

"Sounds good to me." Betty had put on some shorts and a loose T-shirt this time rather than her usual tank top. "What're you in the mood for?" She chuckled, "And don't say hamburgers because I'm sick of burgers and fries."

They wound up at the small cafe on the corner, where home-cooked food was almost as good as what Mom made. At least, that's what the sign outside said, and Betty couldn't argue that point.

"Well? Did it hit the spot?" Deanne asked.

"Sure did." Betty leaned back and inhaled deeply. "It's been a long time since I've had Hawaiian–style chili," she said. "It's good."

"Probably canned," Deanne said with a chuckle. "But I know what you mean." She held up her spoon as if about to say something but then put it back into her bowl and took another bite. Silence fell over them for a few minutes.

Betty was having a hard time leaving her day behind at the office. Images of Mark Diaz kept popping into her mind. There was only one way to purge all thoughts of business. "Wanna go for a walk after we eat?" she asked.

"Sure," Deanne replied. "I'm up for one of your marathon walks. It's been a long time."

They ate quickly, paid their bill, then left. Betty inhaled and let the fresh air that had a fragrance all its own flow into her lungs. Yes, it sure did feel great to be back.

"Something's bothering you," Deanne said bluntly as they stepped off the curb toward the beach.

Betty felt conflicted about what she should say. On the one hand, she wanted to dump all her problems on her friend, but on the other hand, things generally had a way of working out and she didn't want to worry Deanne needlessly.

"It's really nothing important," Betty finally said, figuring it was best not to say anything about her difficult boss yet.

"Okay, but if you wanna talk, I'm all ears." She pointed to the water. "Hey, look, there's a surfer still out on the waves."

It was still light out, but the sun was resting on the horizon. There wasn't much daylight left.

Deanne squinted as she tried to get a better look at the surfer. "He's still too far out. I'm not sure if I know him."

Betty laughed out loud. "You know all the regulars, don't you?"

With a one-shouldered shrug, Deanne bobbed her head around. "Well, maybe a few."

That was an understatement. Based on what Betty remembered, Deanne knew practically everyone who lived within a mile of the beach, plus many of the tourists.

They sat down on the sand and watched the surfer for a few minutes before either of them said a word. There were still a few people lying on towels, but by now, most of the sunbathers had gone home or back to their hotel rooms. This was a peaceful time of day, which allowed Betty to appreciate the majestic beauty of where she was.

"That guy's really good," Deanne noticed. "He's not coming all the way in, so I have no idea who he is." She squinted and leaned forward. "He looks like he's trying to prove something."

"You sure you don't know him?" Betty asked.

Shaking her head, Deanne said, "He looks familiar, but he's still too far away to tell."

"He has a good build," Betty said.

"Yeah, but don't they all?"

That was the truth. Surfing was a great workout.

The salty breeze lifted Betty's spirits as they sat side by side, both facing the ocean, enjoying watching the surfer and appreciating his physique from their safe distance. She'd really missed being able to do this.

Betty could tell Deanne had something on her mind the way she fidgeted and traced circles in the sand with her toe. "What's up, Deanne?" she asked.

"Oh, nothing." Deanne stopped what she was doing and stared out at the surfer for a few seconds before she sighed. "Just Steve."

"Steve?"

"Yeah, he and I have been seeing a little of each other lately."

"That's good, right?"

Deanne paused then said, "I thought so, but he's so nice to everyone, I'm not sure how he feels."

"Have you asked him?"

With a look of pure horror, Deanne shook her head no. "Are you kidding? I could never do that."

Betty laughed. Now she knew why Deanne never stuck with one guy. She was afraid to communicate.

"You might try having a heart-to-heart talk with him," Betty advised. "That way you can clear the air and find out where you stand."

"How's the hunky boss?" Deanne asked, changing the direction of the conversation and blindsiding Betty.

"Um, I guess he's okay."

"I know you're dying to talk about what happened today. Did he say something to upset you?"

"No, not exactly." Betty sniffed. "It's just that I don't think he trusts me."

"Do you think there's a reason?"

"Probably. No one's said anything outright, but based on what I've picked up, the guy in my position before me did some fancy accounting, and they had to force him into retirement."

Deanne cast a glance over at Betty. "He's blaming you for that?"

"I don't think he's blaming me, but he's making me prove myself. And he has this training system that's very basic, but I have to go through each and every step and jump through hoops, even though I know all the stuff in it."

"Have you discussed your feelings with him?" Deanne asked. "You know, clear the air?"

Betty snickered. "You think I should open up?"

Deanne smiled back. "I was just telling you the same thing you told me."

Both of them turned their attention back to the surfer, who'd found a spot where he could catch the next wave. They watched in silence as he waited patiently, then turned at just the right time, stood, and expertly rode the wave until it fizzled. He then got down on his knees and paddled right back to where he was. This guy's endurance was amazing.

The last of the beachgoers had gathered their towels and mats and were heading home, leaving Betty and Deanne alone on the sand. This was the end of another gorgeous Hawaiian day. Too bad Betty had to spend most of her time cooped up in an office with a sour-puss watching over her all week.

Mark was just now beginning to feel the stress lift from his shoulders as he rode the wave until it ended. The beach was virtually empty, with the exception of the two women who'd sat down and were watching him.

Waikiki's waves were nothing to Mark after surfing on the North Shore. But it took a while to get to the other side of the island, and the rush-hour traffic would add to that time. He needed quick relief, and Waikiki was close, so this was where he generally came after work—if it was still daylight.

He caught a few more waves before deciding to quit for the day. Now, maybe he'd be able to sleep.

Mark had been restless lately, and nothing but surfing gave him the ability to relax. And even so, he wasn't totally free of the worries that plagued him.

The state of turmoil at the bank had turned his world upside-down. Until he'd caught Dunstan dipping into the till, he felt like he had the world by the tail. He'd reached his career goals, he had the surf close at hand, and there was always someone new to date. Mark kept his private life separate from business, so he maintained a friendly distance between himself and his co-workers. That was the one piece of advice he'd taken from his father, who never stopped pushing him.

Being the son of a successful businessman gave Mark all the advantages a kid could ask for, growing up. He never had to wait for anything he wanted, but he often felt like there was a hole in his life—something he couldn't put his finger on. After college, Mark tried a few things, jobs that had potential but didn't feel right, then decided to move to Hawaii after nothing else appealed to him. His life was good now, in order, with everything he liked at his fingertips. And then the fiasco with Dunstan.

Mark felt his body tense up as he thought about the previous operations manager, so he forced the incident from his mind. Instead, he focused on the surfing and how those two women sat and watched him as they talked.

He was too far away from them to see for sure, but based on how they moved and carried themselves, he suspected they were college age or older. They both had a confidence about them that let him know they were adults, but they still looked pretty young.

As he paddled all the way to shore, Mark glanced up and saw that the women had left. Good. He didn't feel like talking to anyone, but he hated being rude. Since they'd been watching him for quite a while, he figured he'd have to say a few words to them if they were still there when he left.

Mark lived a couple blocks up from the beach, so he decided to walk home. He stopped at the edge of the sand long enough to pull on his T-shirt and step into his flip-flops, then he turned and headed home, to his small house overlooking the Ala Wai Canal. It wasn't the most plush place in the world, but it was close to everything he needed, and he had a place to keep his boards. He walked almost everywhere he went, but when he needed to drive, his VW Bug suited him just fine. It was easy to strap a board to the roof, and it ran great.

Once he reached his yard, he hoisted his board up

on the stand he'd made. He turned on the faucet, tugged on the hose, and rinsed the board, then dried it off before waxing it down. Mark took good care of his boards because that was basically all he did in his time off besides date very occasionally, which suited him perfectly fine.

So why did he feel so empty and frustrated all the time?

Chapter Four

Steve was back at the house waiting for Deanne. "Where you two been?" he asked, a playful smile twitching the corners of his lips.

Deanne cast a coquettish look right back at him. "We were just doing girl stuff."

Girl stuff? Betty had to smile at that phrase.

"Come here, you," Steve said as he reached out and pulled Deanne to him, then let go as if she'd burned him.

Betty noticed the looks of surprise and wonder on both of their faces. She wondered if they knew they were in love.

Steve smiled at Betty. "So, how's it working with Mark? He's one heck of a guy. Bet your office is loads of fun."

"Yeah," Betty said sarcastically. "Loads."

43

Steve reared back. "You got a problem with Diaz?"

Deanne stepped in to rescue her. "He's not as much fun at the office as he is when he's playing."

"Oh," Steve said, nodding. "So he has a case of boss-itis, huh?"

"I don't know what it is, but he's not the easiest person to work for. But I'm sure I'll get used to him."

Betty was tired of talking about Mr. Diaz. She wanted to take a break from him after being in the same bank with him all day.

Turning to Deanne, Steve said, "I stopped by to see if you wanted to go out for shave ice."

"Sounds good," Deanne said eagerly. "Wanna go, Betty?"

"No, not really. I'm exhausted. You two go ahead and have fun. I think I'll just get ready for bed and read a little."

"You sure?" Deanne's expression was sweet and hopeful, like that of a small child being promised something special.

"Positive."

After they left, Betty did exactly as she said she'd do. She was tired, and she needed a little time to think. Her job wore her out more than it ever had in Arizona, which made no sense. In fact, she should have been able to walk in and start being productive, right from the get-go. If it weren't for Mark Diaz, she would have.

Betty thought of all the ways she could handle the problem. One way, to go around him and speak to his boss, was out of the question if she wanted to continue working in Hawaii. Being savvy in corporate politics, she knew that was the kiss of death to a person's career.

Another thing she could do was have a heart-to-heart talk with him and explain that she knew and understood the systems of the bank and that she wanted the freedom to do her job. But he'd made it clear that she was to follow her training, step-by-step, and then he'd let her do what she'd been hired to do.

Sleep came quickly, but then again so did morning. She groaned as she got out of bed.

"It's not supposed to be that bad," Deanne said.

Betty quickly turned to her roommate. "Sorry I woke you."

"You didn't. I couldn't sleep."

"Wanna talk about it?"

Deanne sat up. "Maybe you and I both need to take a day and just talk."

"Good idea."

"Wanna drive over to Sandy Beach on Saturday?"

Betty nodded. "Yes, I'd like that."

At least knowing she had plans for Saturday made the morning more bearable. Betty quickly got ready for work, ate breakfast, and headed for the bank. As before, she was the second one there. The light was shining beneath the door to Mr. Diaz's office.

Betty tiptoed to her little space. She carefully went inside, turned on her own light, then closed the door behind her. She'd sat down and picked up the printed pages and had engrossed herself in reading them when she heard the knock at her door.

"Ms. Sorenson?"

"Come in, Mr. Diaz."

He turned the knob and walked inside. The sight of this man nearly stole her breath. His navy suit fit him to perfection. The strong chin that jutted over his white-starched collar gave her a window to his stubbornness, but his eyes belied everything. There was a pain, a sensitivity she hadn't noticed before.

"Mind if I sit down?" he asked.

Betty gestured silently toward the chair. She couldn't take her eyes off his face.

"How's it going with the reading?" he asked after a few seconds of awkward silence.

"Okay, I guess." Now was the perfect opportunity to discuss her concerns with him, but she felt a knot forming in her chest.

Mr. Diaz let out a light chuckle. "Based on what I've seen, you're doing extremely well. In fact, I've been doing a little thinking about your position."

"You have?" Was it too much to hope? Betty tried to quell the flutter in her heart.

He steepled his fingers and leaned back, stretching his legs out in front of him. Betty pulled up but quickly forced herself to settle down. She didn't need to be looking at Mark Diaz as a man. He was her boss, for heaven's sake. Her uptight, controlling boss.

"Yes, I have. And I've spoken to the regional manager back on the mainland, and she said you were the one person she could always count on."

There was nothing Betty could do to prevent her heart from hammering. This was sounding better and better by the second.

"So I've decided to let you loose a little at a time. We have some projects that need immediate attention, and I have to go to the Big Island for several days."

Betty almost fell over backward. "Are you serious?" This was a major milestone for her. "When are you leaving?" Oh, man, that came out all wrong.

Instead of anger, Mr. Diaz showed amusement. "Eager to get rid of me, huh? I guess based on the way I've been acting, I can't blame you."

"It's not that—"

Holding up both hands, Mr. Diaz silenced her. "Hey, don't worry about it. I understand you like to be productive, which is precisely why I'm handing you the projects I can't get to right away."

Betty wanted to jump up, run around her desk, and hug the man. But she couldn't. He was not ready for any show of emotion, even if it was strictly due to excitement over her career happiness. This was the type of guy who'd take it the wrong way.

"I'll bring some files in here later on this morning, and I'll E-mail the rest of the information to get you started. Fran can help you, but don't expect too much from her. She started here at a bad time, so she didn't get adequate training."

With a nod, Betty said, "I understand. I've trained

a few office assistants and secretaries. Want me to do the same with Fran?"

Mr. Diaz's jaw tightened. "No, she'll learn the way I train her."

Okay, so he wasn't ready for her suggestions yet, even though it would have made everyone's life so much easier. Well, if he wanted to be that way, Betty would play his game.

"Let me know if you need anything," he said as he stood and headed for the door. His hand was on the knob when he stopped and turned to face her. "By the way, the Hawaiian regional office executives like us to call each other by our first names. They seem to think it makes a friendlier office atmosphere."

It was clear by how he'd said that, Mr. Diaz didn't agree with the Hawaiian office executives. "Is that okay with you?" she asked.

"Of course. Why wouldn't it be?" He looked her in the eye as if to challenge her.

Betty glanced down then back at him. "No reason . . . Mark."

He forced a smile. "Thanks, Betty. See you in a little while, after I pull all those files together. Keep reading your training material so we can resume that once I get back."

After he left, Betty dropped her head on the desk and started to laugh silently, until she realized she seemed half crazy. She didn't know if she should shout with joy or scream with frustration. Mark Diaz was handing her something with one hand while taking it away with the other. She despised office games, but it appeared she'd have to play them with him.

At the regular starting time, Fran popped her head into Betty's office. "Need anything, Ms. Sorenson?"

"Not now, Fran. Please call me Betty."

With a smile, the secretary nodded. "Okay, Betty. Mr. Diaz told me we'd be working on some projects while he was on the Big Island."

Betty was confused. Was the first-name thing only for executives or for everyone? She wasn't sure if Fran was the right person to ask, but she took a chance.

"Is there a reason you don't use first names, Fran?"

"Not really. We're supposed to be a friendly bank and all, but Mr. Dunstan didn't like the first-name policy, so I got in the habit of being more formal, since he was my boss."

"Oh, I see," Betty said.

"Is that all for now? I haven't gotten my coffee yet, and I can't think straight yet."

"Go ahead and get your coffee then. I'll let you know when I need something." Hopefully, Fran had something constructive to do.

Betty did some speed reading through the training material. She would have taken her time if she didn't already know what was printed. It was basic, but she had to admit, it was good and well organized.

Mark stopped by with boxes. "I have more in my office," he told her. "Where do you want me to put this?"

She looked around her tiny office then decided it

would be best to stick it behind the credenza. "How about there?" she asked as she pointed. "I'll help you with the rest."

As Betty walked back to Mark's office, she was well aware of the glances they got from the other bank operations staff. And she didn't miss the hidden smirks on some of their faces. Either Mark had a reputation, or these people didn't have enough to do. She was sure she'd find out eventually, probably soon if she was right about human nature.

Once they had all the boxes transferred from Mark's office to hers, he stood up, brushed his hands off, and smiled down at her. Her heart thudded.

"Sorry about that," he said softly.

Could he hear what was going on inside her? Not possible.

"After what happened with Dunstan, everyone here expects more excitement to follow."

Oh, now she understood. He was apologizing for everyone's behavior.

"That's okay. I can handle it."

Mark lifted one corner of his lips. "Yes, I'm sure you can."

He spent the afternoon giving her explicit instructions about what he wanted done on the projects. Betty knew instantly she could do this with one hand tied behind her back, but she didn't tell him that. She'd play his game and eventually she'd win his confidence.

That afternoon, when she got home, Deanne tilted

her head and looked at her. "Something's different," she said. "Did you have a good day at the office, or did you decide to play hooky?"

Betty chuckled. "My day at work was okay, but not great. I'm making progress, though."

"That's good. Oh, I hope you don't mind if I don't eat dinner with you. Steve's taking me to the North Shore. He just bought some new boards for his shop up there, and he asked me to ride along." She paused and studied Betty. "That is, unless you need to talk."

Betty waved her hand. She'd welcome the time alone. "I might be your roommate, but I don't have to be with you every second I'm not working."

As soon as Deanne left, Betty raided the refrigerator. She'd bought a bunch of easy-to-fix meal items, so she managed to put together a plate filled with smoked fish, salad, and fresh fruit. Perfect for eating on the front porch.

After dinner, Betty decided to head over to the beach so she could clear her head. As she arrived, she saw that surfer from the day before. She sat down on the sand and watched him ride the waves for nearly an hour, tirelessly timing each one, gliding along the glistening crest, then paddling back out for more of the same. There was a certain comforting, predictable peace to what he was doing, and Betty had a fleeting desire to change her resolve about surfing. Maybe Steve was right; maybe it would be good for her.

A few times, it appeared that the surfer was watching her, too, but she didn't want to think about that.

She wasn't doing anything nearly as interesting as what he was doing.

Then, suddenly, when he had his focus on something on the beach, a wave came up from behind and clobbered him. Betty stood up to get a better look. He didn't appear for several seconds, and during that time, her heart stood still. The man had been wiped out. *Please, please come up for air*, she willed.

She felt an overwhelming sense of relief when the man surfaced, slapping at his board and obviously frustrated and possibly embarrassed. At least he was alive. If he had any sense, he'd come on in and let it go for the night. But he didn't. He seemed more determined than ever to ride the next wave. She noticed he was favoring his left hand, but he seemed to manage okay without using it too much. Occasionally, he lifted his right hand and slicked his hair back. It must have been habit because his close-cropped hair wasn't long enough to get in his eyes.

Betty replayed the surfer's accident in her mind, which reinforced why she'd never be foolish enough to get hooked on surfing. Those people were the most stubborn and obsessed people she'd ever known in her life.

Although she wanted to head on back home, Betty felt compelled to stick around the beach until the surfer decided to call it a day. She had to wait another half hour before she saw him paddling to shore. Once his feet hit the sand, she stood up and walked home.

* * *

Mark wanted to kick himself for not paying attention. He knew better than to stare at the pretty woman on the beach, but he couldn't seem to take his eyes off her. She moved with such fluid grace, he was mesmerized by her from the moment he'd first laid eyes on her.

And she reminded him of someone, but he couldn't put his finger on whom. Speaking of fingers, he had to do something about that gash. Fortunately, the board had just grazed his finger and not clobbered something more critical.

The next morning, Mark had to finish everything in the Honolulu office before boarding the plane for the Big Island. Betty was there when he arrived, which was a first for him. He always liked being in the office ahead of everyone else because he felt more in control.

She seemed eager to take instructions, so he told her more than he'd intended. "Great," she said. "I'll have all this done when you get back. By the way, when will you be getting back?"

"Next week, probably by Wednesday."

He squinted. The sun was streaming in through the window behind her, so he couldn't see her features as well as usual. However, her silhouette was clear, and there was something that reminded him of something he couldn't quite remember.

"What happened to your finger?" she asked, pointing to the heavy bandage he had rested on the desk.

"Accident. I did something stupid."

Betty nodded. "Oh."

Mark felt like a jerk for giving her such a blunt answer, but he didn't want to tell her he'd turned his back on one of Hawaii's famous waves. That's what beginners did, and he was definitely no beginner. He'd even considered making a career of surfing before he realized his father would disown him if he did.

Raking his fingers through his hair, Mark stood up. "I guess it's time to leave things in your hands, Betty. Think you can handle it?"

She gave him a curious look then nodded. "Oh, I think I can handle this. If you need something else, just call, and I'll see what I can do."

What was it about Mark that seemed so familiar? She'd never met him before she'd started her new job.

He'd raked his fingers through his hair, something he didn't have much of. On a hunch, Betty punched the intercom button. Fran's voice was quick. "Yes, Betty? You need something?"

"Could you come in here for a second, Fran?"

A loud "click" sounded, then next thing Betty knew, Fran was standing at the door. "Whatcha need?"

"Has Mark's hair always been this short?" Betty asked.

The second those words were out of her mouth, she realized how she sounded. She wanted to crawl under her desk and hide.

Fran didn't seem to mind the senseless question, though. "No, as a matter of fact, he had longer hair until we had to deal with Mr. Dunstan and the possibility of going to court."

"I see," Betty said as the picture started coming together. "Thanks, Fran."

"Why do you ask?"

She should have known better than to think she'd get off without an explanation. "He reminds me of someone I knew back in Arizona," Betty said.

"I know what you mean," Fran said without missing a beat, talking a mile-a-minute like she seemed to do most of the time. "I'm always seeing people who remind me of someone I used to know, but most of the time, I never saw them before in my life. You know how we're supposed to have a twin somewhere in this world, someone who looks just like us?"

Betty didn't know anything about that, but she figured it would be easiest to nod and let Fran's chatter run its course without any help from her.

"Maybe you knew his twin."

"Maybe. Thanks, Fran."

"If you need to know anything about anyone here, just buzz me. I know a bunch of stuff about everyone."

Betty just bet she did. Probably not much got by Fran.

Well, I'll be, Betty thought as she sat and stared at the files on her blotter. She already knew Mark Diaz was a surfer because Deanne had told her, but she didn't think about him going to the beach after work. In her mind, he was the type to go home and crunch numbers for hours before going to the gym for a work-out.

He was an incredible surfer, too. Until his one major wipeout, he had full command of the waves. That finger of his must hurt, yet he managed to get through a day in the office without complaining. What a man. Betty chuckled to herself. A new light had been shed on her boss.

Mark left the office early to catch his flight to the Big Island. Betty immersed herself in the projects he'd left her to do, but she decided to pace herself rather than do them at the speed she knew she could. Having nothing to do before he returned would be one of the worst things that could happen, not to mention put a strain on their business relationship.

That afternoon, Deanne wasn't in the house when she arrived. She decided to take her walk to the beach before dinner then stop off and pick up some fast-food on the way home.

As she expected, there was no surfer at sunset tonight. With a smile, Betty sat and watched the waves as she contemplated her move and realized that things were never as they seemed. Mark Diaz had proven that, simply by being the office ogre by day and the frustrated surfer by night. She remembered one of the first comments Deanne made a couple nights ago when she said the surfer looked like he was trying to prove something. Now Betty realized that wasn't what he was doing. He was trying to work out his frustrations.

Now she wondered if she might be contributing to his stress. Until now, that thought hadn't occurred to her.

On her way to the house, Betty picked up a bag of chicken tenders and some fries, hoping Deanne would be there to help her eat them. And she was. To Betty's dismay, Deanne's eyes were puffy, apparently from crying.

Chapter Five

Betty set the food on the kitchen table then went back into the living room, where Deanne still sat on the sofa, staring at the wall. "Wanna talk about what happened?" Betty asked.

Deanne paused, started to shake her head, then licked her lips. "We can't communicate."

"Who?" Betty asked. "You and Steve?"

With a nod, Deanne started to sob then caught herself. She pulled her lips between her teeth and looked directly at Betty. "He's very nice to me."

"Then what's the problem?"

"Steve is nice to everyone. I don't have any idea if he thinks I'm special, or if I'm just another person to be nice to."

Betty had to hold back her smile. Although Deanne's behavior would seem strange to someone who didn't know and understand Deanne, Betty knew exactly what was bothering Deanne.

Deanne had always been one of those people that everyone was attracted to—both men and women. Her bubbly personality and quick wit were matched by her extreme intelligence. She was athletic, fun, and pretty—every guy's dream. But in the past, she bounced from one guy to another, including Betty's brother Jeff. He'd liked her, but he told Betty there was no chemistry, so he didn't see the point in pursuing a deeper relationship with her. Betty kept that to herself and let Jeff and Deanne work it out.

But for now, the issue wasn't Jeff. Steve was the man breaking Deanne's heart.

"Why don't you just come out and ask him?" Betty advised. "You've known him for years, and you've been his most valuable employee."

"I know. And I don't want to ruin our working relationship."

This was definitely a problem that she'd have to work through herself. Betty stood up. "I brought some chicken home if you want some."

Deanne joined her for dinner. She seemed to feel a little bit better, which was a relief to Betty.

"So, how'd it go with Mark today?"

"You're not gonna believe this."

"What? You and Mark are now bosom buddies, and he confided all his deepest, darkest secrets to you in the break room?"

Betty laughed. Leave it to Deanne to think of something so outlandish. "Not quite. But close. Remember that surfer from that night we sat on the beach?"

"Yeah." Deanne nodded, but her expression was still blank.

"That was Mark."

Deanne looked stunned, then she burst out laughing. "You're right, it was. I knew he looked familiar. What'd he say when you told him you were watching."

"I didn't."

"And why not?" Deanne asked.

"The opportunity didn't present itself."

"Maybe you should take your own advice and try open communication."

"Touché."

With a chuckle, Deanne said, "I thought you might like that. Look at us, Betty. Here we are, two reasonably attractive, intelligent women, and we're acting like young girls who don't know how to act around men."

"Speak for yourself. I know."

"Okay." Deanne bit into a chicken tender and chewed before adding, "What should we do now?"

"I wish I knew."

"Do you like Mark?"

"Are you nuts? He's my boss."

"Yeah, I know, but he is cute. And once you get to know him, he's one of the nicest guys around."

"I'll have to take your word for that, Deanne."

"You'll see it soon."

"It'll be a while before I even see him again. He left for the Big Island and won't be back until next week."

Deanne frowned. "What about that training program he has you on?"

"He put me on the fast track, and now I'm actually doing projects that are productive."

"See? He knows genius when he sees it."

Again, Betty laughed. "No, I think it was more a matter of desperation."

"Whatever works."

Mark had just landed on Hawaii, the Big Island, and he was waiting for his shuttle when the image of Betty Sorenson flashed through his mind. She'd been watching him all morning, looking at his bandaged finger and acting strange. Something had changed.

He sure hoped he hadn't made a huge mistake starting her on the project before she finished her training. The last thing he needed was a botched assignment he'd have to undo and take care of himself.

All afternoon and evening, Mark worried about Betty and how she'd handle her first project without him being there for support and questions. He called Nancy, the person he was still training on the Big Island. She said she'd see him first thing in the morning because she had plans for the night.

That set him on edge. Mark had flown in to work with her, and every minute counted. Nancy knew he was coming. He wouldn't have thought he'd have to tell her to schedule her time around him while he was there. Mark was a very busy man.

At least he'd brought some work to do and his laptop. He could send some E-mails to the office, and they'd get them first thing in the morning. Then he grabbed the stack of papers from his briefcase and started going over them, planning how he'd spend his time with Nancy in the morning. Hopefully, she'd catch on and he wouldn't have to stay more than a few days.

The next morning, Mark had to wait fifteen minutes, Nancy was late. She offered an apologetic smile. "Sorry, but my husband and I were out late last night. Let's get started."

Mark had to put his own frustrations aside as he laid everything out in front of her. By noon, she was more confused than ever. Mark wanted to rip everything up and start over.

"I don't understand any of this," Nancy told him. "Why is it so complicated?"

"It's not," he said with an exasperated sigh. He wanted to tell her she wasn't paying attention, or she'd understand. But he didn't. Instead, he forced a smile and said, "Let me go call my new trainee back in Honolulu, and we can start over."

Betty answered as soon as Fran put him through. He was relieved to know she was at her desk working on the project.

"Any questions?" he asked.

"Nope. Everything's clear as a bell here," she said. "How's it going with you?"

Mark felt compelled to tell her how frustrated he was. "I'm sure it's me," he said. "I've tried explaining everything about the task, but she still doesn't get it."

"Mind if I talk to her?" Betty asked.

An alarm sounded in Mark's head, but he quickly decided it was pointless to act on it. Besides, Betty and Nancy were bound to meet eventually, anyway. "Okay, that's fine."

He put Nancy on and left the office to find some coffee. When he came back, Nancy had a huge smile on her face, and her eyes were twinkling. "I finally got it, Mark. I understand what you've been trying to explain."

"You do?" Mark was doubtful, but he hoped she was right.

"Yes, Betty was very patient and walked me through it."

"She did?"

Nancy offered an enthusiastic nod. "It's really quite simple." Then she told him how Betty had explained it.

By golly, she'd nailed it.

"Uh, Nancy, this is great."

"No," Nancy argued. "Betty's the one who's great." She crinkled her forehead as she glanced out the window, and thought for a moment then turned back to Mark. "Her name sounds very familiar. How long's she been working for you?"

"Not long. About a week. Maybe you met her when you went to the regional meeting."

Nancy lit up. "That's right. Betty Sorenson from Arizona. Did you know she gave an entire seminar on corporate ethics and bank operations?"

"She did?" Mark had no idea. Betty must have been more savvy than he realized.

"Yes. In fact, she was introduced as one of the most promising young women to have come through First Guardian's management training program."

Why hadn't someone told him? Mark felt like he'd been played a fool.

"Nancy, since you have it all figured out now, why don't you get started on this project? I'll be in my office if you need me. I have a few phone calls to make."

"Sure thing," she said in a very perky voice. Way too perky to suit him.

Mark called his counterpart in California and asked about Betty Sorenson. He got an earful, all about how this woman was incredible and how she'd most likely run the entire operation within just a few years if she was given free reign. His call only made him feel more foolish than before.

He buried his face in his hands as he tried to figure out how to turn things around and still save face. Betty must be laughing all over the place at how elementary his training program was when she could have written the entire thing in her sleep.

Mark ran some numbers on his computer, trying to

get his mind off his gaffe, but he couldn't stop thinking about it. He was startled by the sound of someone clearing her throat. With a quick glance up, he saw Nancy standing in the doorway.

"Need something?"

Smiling, Nancy nodded. "I've got an idea, but you probably won't go for it."

"What's that?"

"Not that I think you'll do it. But I was just thinking. Is it possible to bring Betty Sorenson over to this office? I'd love to meet her and pick her brain. She's brilliant, according to the grapevine, and I'm sure I could learn something valuable from her."

Funny, Mark had just been thinking the same thing. He knew he had a lot to learn.

"It's possible," he said.

"Really?" Nancy folded her hands beneath her chin. "That would be so cool."

Yes, he agreed. It would be very cool. Maybe if he brought Betty over, he'd have some free time at the end of every day to catch some of the waves this island was known for.

"Okay, I'll do it."

The way Nancy was acting you would have thought a celebrity was coming to pay her a personal visit. Or maybe Betty was a celebrity, and no one had told him.

Nancy was married, so he didn't ask her to join him for a business dinner. Instead, Mark chose to order room service, then end the night going over financial reports. He wanted to call Betty, but he figured it would be better to wait until morning and call her at the office rather than call her at home. She deserved a little personal time.

Since Mark had been given the authority to do whatever he needed to do in order to get the job done, he wasn't concerned about consulting higher-ups. He'd made sure the Honolulu branch was caught up, so once Betty finished the projects he'd assigned her, she'd be free to join him on the Big Island. Knowing what he now knew about her, she'd be finished soon, so it wouldn't be long.

Mark fell asleep thinking about Betty and how competent he'd discovered she was. She was champing at the bit to do more work, but he'd held her back. Stupid move on his part.

At least now he knew. Betty was capable of doing her job and probably his. Mark chuckled. This was good. Very good. Now he'd be able to take a much needed vacation he'd postponed the last couple of years because he was worried about the job getting done. Some people had called him a power freak, but that wasn't the case. From his vantage point, he had a valid case. There was no one in any of the Hawaii offices who could cover all bases for very long.

Mark's dreams that night strayed from professionalism. He imagined walking with Betty, side by side, hand in hand, on the beach. The sun was setting, and he felt a peace unlike any he'd ever felt in his life.

Then the sound of the alarm clock startled him out of his sleep. Good thing, too, or he'd have kissed those glistening lips, and he might never be able to face Betty Sorenson again.

He could hardly wait to get to the office and call her. Hopefully, she wouldn't ask too many questions.

She didn't. In fact, she didn't even sound surprised when he told her he'd have tickets waiting for her at the airport.

"Sure, boss, I'll be there. What time?"

No questions. No argument. No explanation. Nothing. Just compliance. There had to be a catch.

Mark told her he'd have to make arrangements and call her back. She said that was fine.

All the details were taken care of in a matter of minutes. Betty took down the information and said she'd finish what she was working on and she'd be right there.

"Do you need more time?" he asked.

"No, I finished the projects you assigned," she replied. "I was just writing a report covering the rest of the training so you'd know I read it."

"Uh, good job, Betty. See you in a few hours."

"Fine."

"I'll pick you up at the airport."

"No need. I can rent a car and drive."

Mark was appalled at that. "No, I'll pick you up." Then he realized he needed an excuse. "We have a few things to discuss before you come into the branch, so we can talk in the car."

She hesitated before she sighed. "Okay, I'll see you soon, Mark."

Her voice made a mess of Mark's insides. He leaned back and cupped his hand over his mouth as he thought about Betty Sorenson. After a few minutes, he smiled. It had been a very long time since he'd been challenged by anyone, let alone a beautiful woman. And she didn't even know she was challenging him.

Mark picked up his pen and started making notes. He'd wanted to try surfing here on the Big Island, but he hadn't had the opportunity yet. Ever since he'd been coming here, he'd wanted to try his hand at the waves here, which broke over very rocky shores. Most of them weren't quite as challenging as those on Oahu, but he saw the danger of hitting the lava rocks as being a new experience. He had to be careful, or the rocks would tear him apart.

Somewhere in all this, Mark knew, was a parallel to what was going on between him and Betty. He still needed to figure it all out.

Betty stared at the phone she still held in her hand. Was she really going to the Big Island in a couple of hours? She shook her head as she returned the phone to the cradle. This was really strange. One day her boss was running her through a training program she didn't need, and the next day, he said he needed her to help explain the complex concepts to the employees at the Big Island branch. She was definitely missing a piece of the puzzle.

As much as she wanted to figure it all out, she didn't have time, she realized as she glanced at her watch.

She dialed Fran's extension and told her what was going on and said she'd call and let her know what was going on. Fran sounded very happy, as usual, and not at all surprised.

Then she went home to pack. Deanne had stopped by the house during her lunch break. "Hey, Betty. What're you doing home now? Decide to take early retirement?"

"I wish. No, Mark called from the Hilo office and said he wanted me to come over for a while."

Deanne's eyebrows shot up. "You're kidding, right?"

"No, I'm serious as a judge." Betty couldn't look Deanne in the eye. She had a feeling she knew what her roommate was thinking—that something more than a business relationship was going on between her and Mark.

"This should be very interesting," Deanne said.

Definitely time to change the subject. "So, how's Steve?"

Deanne flopped over on the sofa. "Why'd you have to ask? I haven't seen him all day."

"It's only noon."

"Yeah, I know, but time drags when I don't hear from him."

"Have you thought about calling him? He has a cell phone, doesn't he?"

"Of course. But I can't call him unless I need him for something important."

"And why not?"

Deanne rolled her eyes. "Chasing men is not my style, Betty. You know that."

"Oh, yeah, that's right. Sitting around and moping is what you do best. Not! Get up and call Steve, or I'll do it for you."

"Don't you dare," Deanne said as she jumped to her feet. "Maybe I'll call him later, now that I know you're leaving and I won't have anyone to eat dinner with."

"Why don't you call him and ask him over to-night?" Betty advised. "I don't know how long I'll be gone, so you better do it soon."

Deanne nodded. "Okay, I'll do that. But I need to think of a reason or he'll think I'm desperate."

"That's ridiculous."

Betty understood Deanne pretty well. After all, they'd known each other for nearly six years, and they'd been through quite a bit with each other, in-cluding both of them falling in and out of love. She'd never known Deanne to act this way, which led her to believe this time might be different.

On her way out the door, Betty said, "Do it now, Deanne. I don't want you to miss out on this great opportunity."

She heard the sound of Deanne's laughter as she made her way to the street. She still hadn't bought a car, so she had to roll her suitcase down the street to the bus stop, where she'd catch a ride to the airport. Fortunately, it wasn't hard to get around the island, but she still needed a car. She'd have to see about getting one when she got back.

The flight was short—an island hopper—so she was on and off the plane so quickly she didn't have time for even a drink. As soon as she left the gate, she spotted Mark standing off to the side, waiting for her.

Betty stopped and stared at him, taking advantage of the fact that he hadn't seen her yet. The man was breathtakingly handsome, in his lightweight wool blend suit, his hair cut to perfection, his dark features sharp and angled. If he weren't her boss, she'd seriously consider making a play for him. As it was, he was off limits.

Chapter Six

Betty felt the thud to her chest when their gazes met. She quickly glanced away to regain her balance, then she turned back to him with a smile.

"Thanks for meeting me here, Mark." She had to clear her throat.

He licked his lips and took her bag. "Thanks for coming on such short notice."

Was it her imagination, or had the air between them just become even more tense than before? Betty couldn't have imagined that was possible, but it certainly seemed that way. It had been a very long time since she'd been speechless, and she felt that way now.

"We'll go straight to the hotel so you can freshen up. I'll wait for you in the lobby."

Betty started to tell him they could get right to work

if that would be better, but she decided it might be best to go to her room and be alone to regroup for a few minutes before going to the bank with him. "Good idea."

He'd gotten her a room at one of the nicest hotels she'd ever seen. The lobby was open, with a light breeze blowing through, the sound of soft chimes filling the air. She inhaled deeply and noticed the floral scent, probably coming from one of the lobby gift shops.

Mark handed her bag to a bellman, and she followed right behind. The man made sure everything was satisfactory, then left her alone. Betty squeezed her eyes shut and took a deep breath. Her new position with the bank had been full of surprises from day one—at first from how little confidence her boss had in her and now the total opposite. She'd been back and forth on the scale of frustration, and now she didn't know what to think.

After freshening her makeup and running a comb through her hair, Betty took a quick glance in the mirror to make sure she still looked professional, then she left her room to meet Mark back in the lobby. He was standing, facing the elevator when the door opened.

"Hi," he said. "That was quick." His gaze raked her from head to toe, then he looked her in the eye. "Ready to face some new associates?"

"That's why I'm here, right?"

Since Betty had no idea how Mark had explained her visit, she'd decided to keep a low profile and let him do all the talking until she had a better handle on the situation. She was surprised when he came right out and said, "This is Betty Sorenson. She's one of the finest operations managers in First Guardian's system."

Her face felt hot and flushed as she stumbled over her own greeting, after the flattering introduction. Mark stood by and smiled with pride. As they walked through the lobby of the bank and made their way to the operations offices, she took several deep breaths to get over her latest surprise.

Nancy gushed over her, making her even more uncomfortable. "I'm so glad to finally meet you, Betty. I've heard such wonderful things about you."

"You have?" Betty asked, turning toward Mark.

He shrugged. "It's all stuff we heard from your office in Arizona."

After an hour of introductions, Betty managed to assist Nancy with several things that Mark hadn't been able to get through to her. Nancy listened and nodded as she caught on to what Betty was saying. Mark stood nearby and listened, not saying a word.

An intern hovered nearby, asking occasional questions and offering his own suggestions, which Betty complimented for his astute awareness. "You'll do great when you're finished with school. I hope you plan to work for First Guardian."

The guy's chest puffed out, and he squared his shoulders. "I'd like to."

Betty turned to Mark and nodded. "I hope you seriously consider him for a future position."

"Uh, yes, of course," Mark said awkwardly.

With an instant realization that she might have overstepped her bounds, Betty took a step back. She'd only been working for Mark for a week, and here she was telling him what to do. Her timing was off.

Finally, after the bank had closed and most of the support staff had left, Mark glanced at his watch. "I guess we'd better let Nancy get home. Her husband's probably worried about her."

Nancy grabbed her purse and backed toward the door. "See you in the morning, Betty?"

"I'll be here."

Now, Betty found herself alone with Mark in this big, now-darkened bank building. The only lights were security lights and the one over by the door.

"Got plans for dinner?" he asked.

Betty smiled. "Considering the fact that I didn't even know I was coming here until this morning, I haven't had a chance to make any plans."

"I know a pretty good place if you like Japanese food."

"I love Japanese food," she said a little too quickly. Betty wanted to kick herself in the backside for sounding way too eager.

"Good. It's a couple miles from here, so we'll have to drive."

Betty was impressed that Mark knew Japanese dishes as well as she did. They decided to each order something different and share. Maybe it was an intimate thing to do, but he'd suggested it, and she wasn't about to turn him down.

After dinner, they walked outside and stood in front of the restaurant talking. "Wanna go for a walk?" Mark asked. "It's really nice out, and after a meal like that, a walk would do us good."

"Sure," Betty said.

Mark's arm brushed hers as they walked side by side toward the beach. Her skin tingled where they touched. For a second, she wondered if he felt it, too.

Then suddenly, Mark stopped, touched her arm, and gently turned her to face him. His eyes were filled with wonder and amazement, which was how she felt being with him in this setting.

The hand that was still touching her arm moved, and she leaned toward him. He let out a low groan. "Betty," he said softly before he reached out with both hands and laid them on her shoulders. She shuddered.

As they came together, their gazes locked, Betty knew this kiss would be something she'd never forget. His lips touched hers, and she wrapped her arms around his neck for a long, lingering kiss.

Just as suddenly as he'd touched her, Mark pulled away. He glanced at his watch and looked in the direction of the setting sun as he cleared his throat. "I hope you don't mind if I bring you back to your hotel, but I sort of have plans for the rest of the evening."

She reached up and nervously brushed the side of her hair away from her face. "Of course I don't mind.

I brought some paperwork to do, so don't worry about me."

They began to walk, not mentioning what had just happened. Betty knew she needed to forget about the kiss, but she knew it would be the most difficult thing she'd ever done.

Mark had stopped in his tracks, looked down at her, and smiled. Her heart fluttered, but she bit her lip to redirect her emotions. This unexpected attraction to her boss wasn't healthy if she wanted to advance her career—and she definitely did.

"You wait here," he said after a few more seconds. "I'll get the car."

Betty was thankful for the wait as she stood standing, staring at the horizon. It was different from Oahu. She already knew the island was much bigger, but she hadn't realized it wasn't as crowded. It was much too intimate for her, right now, with her mind where it never should have gone.

Mark arrived with the car, and she got in. They hardly spoke at all on the drive back to her hotel.

"Thanks again, Betty," he said. "When we get back to Honolulu, I'll have to revamp your training program. It's obvious to me now that you need a more advanced system."

What she needed was a good book—something to get her mind off Mark's dark brown eyes, tan face, and broad shoulders. And most of all, his kiss. She'd never felt this way after a kiss before.

There was something else about him, too. Although

he'd acted like a grouch when she'd first met him, she saw a softer side—a side that welcomed suggestions and wasn't too proud to accept her competence in banking. This surprised her, but then she reminded herself, Mark was full of surprises.

She fumbled through the rest of her training paperwork, picked up her novel and tried to read a few pages, then gave up and flipped on the television. Nothing but the news. Oh well. She turned it off and flopped over on the bed. Now that she was alone with her thoughts, maybe she could make some sense of what she was feeling now.

Somewhere between her initial disgust with his lack of confidence in her and his sudden surge of relying on her expertise, she'd noticed Mark Diaz as a man. When she allowed herself to completely let go, she even remembered the image of him on his surfboard in the dusk as he conquered the waves.

Mark Diaz was one complicated, complex man. It was almost as if he were two people—at the office, an uptight business executive with control issues, and at night a relaxed devil-may-care surfer whose only goal was to catch the next wave. If she wanted to be honest with herself, she had to admit to liking both sides of this man.

She knew her brother Jeff would tease her about liking the challenge of trying to solve this puzzle. Maybe there was something to that, but she knew her attraction went even beyond figuring him out. She liked strong men who were able to open up and let her show her skills and talents, which Mark had done today. However, she couldn't get the way he'd acted before out of her mind.

The next morning, Betty was the first one at the bank. Since she didn't have a key, she stood outside on the sidewalk, waiting, which wasn't so bad. The cool morning breeze lifted her spirits and once again made her glad she'd returned to Hawaii.

Nancy was the first familiar face to join her. Betty had waited outside while several other bank employees passed and let themselves in. She didn't want to be cooped up any longer than necessary, since she suspected she wouldn't be seeing the outside for several hours today.

"Where's Mark?" Nancy asked.

Betty lifted one shoulder and let it drop, as if Mark had been the furthest thing from her mind. "He didn't say what time he was coming in."

"He's generally here before me. C'mon, let's get our coffee and see if you can teach me everything I need to know by the time he arrives."

"Sounds like a plan." Betty was happy to be busy rather than wait for Mark, since he was obviously not as concerned about punctuality on the Big Island as he was back in Honolulu. She had no idea why, but several thoughts had crossed her mind like maybe he was seeing someone here, which was why she needed to keep her wits and not get silly notions about him.

They'd been sitting in Nancy's office for more than an hour before Mark showed his face. Betty glanced up when she saw his shadow, but she quickly averted her gaze. She couldn't look him in the eye, not after the thoughts she'd had between last night and this morning.

"Sorry I'm so late," he said as he limped into the room.

"What happened?"

Betty was grateful for Nancy asking, since she was dying to know but didn't want to be the nosy one. She turned and looked to see his response.

Rather than give her a straightforward answer, he shook his head. "Just had a little accident, that's all. Don't worry about it."

Betty nodded then forced herself to focus on what she and Nancy had started. She felt Mark's watchful eye as she went over every last detail, with Nancy making happy sounds about finally "getting it." Betty was relieved that Nancy didn't seem to notice anything different about her relationship with Mark.

Mark ran off for lunch, saying he had an appointment, leaving Betty alone with Nancy. They had a quick sandwich at Nancy's desk, since Betty said she was eager to finish her work so she could get back to Honolulu.

"Maybe we can surprise Mark and finish up today," Nancy said.

"I certainly hope so."

Betty wasn't thrilled with spending another evening alone in her hotel room with nowhere to go and no one to talk to. After Mark pulled away from their kiss, she knew he'd avoid being alone with her again. She decided to really put Nancy's new knowledge to the test and began to challenge her. To both of their surprise, Nancy had an excellent grasp on all of it.

"Well, that about covers it," Betty said as she stood up, rubbing her neck. "I wonder where Mark is. He never came back from lunch, did he?"

"I'm sure he probably did." Nancy leaned over and punched in a number on her phone. Betty heard her ask her secretary if Mark was in the building.

From the way Nancy was responding, Betty knew something was wrong. After she got off the phone, Nancy turned to her and said, "Looks like our boss is already back on Oahu."

That was odd. He should have at least stopped by and said something. "Why didn't he tell us?"

"Apparently, he stuck his head in here and saw that we were doing just fine without him, and he didn't want to interrupt. He left word that you can go back whenever you're finished."

Betty's heart dropped, but she couldn't let on. "I guess I should call and make arrangements to head back tonight."

"My secretary said she'd take care of that when you know for sure. Would you like to stay another day?"

"No, I don't think so. I'd like to get on with my training so I can start actually doing the job I was hired to do."

Nancy chuckled. "Mark is so much like my husband, I sometimes forget they're two different men."

"What do you mean by that?"

"They both want to be in control of everything around them, even when they don't need to be. They worry about the smallest details, and they don't rest until every 'I' is dotted and every 'T' is crossed."

Betty was in full agreement with Nancy, but she wasn't nearly as outspoken. She just smiled back and said, "I'll have to remember that in the future."

"Oh, I'm sure you won't forget it."

The two women smiled at each other. They were in the same boat in their jobs, except Betty wasn't sure how much Nancy's career meant to her, while her own was everything. She loved this bank and everything they stood for. They prided themselves on doing good, clean business, which gave the investors peace of mind.

Nancy's secretary efficiently booked Betty on an early evening flight, and Nancy drove her to the airport so she wouldn't have to get a shuttle. Her plane landed, and the first thing she did was head straight for the bus area.

"Betty!"

She quickly looked up at the sound of Mark's voice. No, it couldn't be. As he came limping toward her, she realized she hadn't imagined it. He really was there.

"What are you doing here, Mark?" Betty asked.

"I came to pick you up. Nancy called me and read me the riot act." He chuckled. "That woman's a real fireball."

Betty tilted her head as she studied Mark. She'd obviously been wrong about the man, since she would have thought he'd be angry at Nancy for fussing at him.

"I hope you don't mind my car," he said as he led the way to the short-term parking. She wanted to say something about his limping, but she wasn't sure if she should ask questions after his brush-off earlier.

"At least you have a car," Betty said. "I've been taking the bus since I've been back here."

"So I heard. You'll have to do something about that." He opened the door to his Bug and then went around to his side and got in. "If you're interested in a great deal on a used car, I have a friend in the business."

"I'm very interested," Betty said.

"Tell you what. If you're not busy Saturday afternoon, I'll stop by and pick you up. He told me that if I knew anyone who needed wheels, he'd give my friends a discount."

Betty nodded as he drove toward her house. She started to give him directions, but then she realized he seemed to know exactly where he was going.

"Do you know where I live?" she asked.

He glanced at her before turning back to the road. A sheepish grin played at his mouth. "Well, yeah."

"How?"

"I looked it up in personnel records."

"Why?"

With a shrug, he replied, "Curious, I guess."

"Oh."

"I hope you don't mind. I promise I won't stalk you."

Betty smiled back at him. "That's a comforting re-assurance."

"I thought it would be." Mark chuckled as he drove several miles in silence.

Finally, Betty couldn't stand it anymore. She had to know what had happened to cause Mark to limp. So what if he got irritated with her. They'd be right back to where they'd started, and she'd mind her own business long enough for him to forget about it.

Pointing to his leg, she said, "Wanna talk about your leg?"

He sucked in a breath and slowly let it out. Betty thought he might blow his stack for a moment, but instead he just shook his head. "I couldn't handle the rocks on the Big Island."

She tensed her forehead as she tried to figure out the puzzle here. "Run that by me again?"

"I was surfing, and I lost control. When I tried to get my footing, I forgot where I was, and I got clobbered by all the rock near the shore."

"When did that happen?"

"Last night, after I brought you back to your hotel, right after dinner."

"You went surfing?"

"Yeah. I like surfing in the early morning or early evening."

Betty's heart lifted, and she felt giddy, which she

tried to squelch. She should never allow moods to come and go, based on light-hearted conversations with any man, especially her boss.

"Did you go to a doctor?" She forced her voice to stay even, rather than let him see she had any feelings, one way or another.

He nodded. "I went to the emergency room, and they put some stuff on it, bandaged it up, and said for me to see my doctor as soon as possible. That's why I came back early."

"What did your doctor say?" Betty wished she could keep her mouth shut, but she was so good at being maternal.

Mark reached over and patted her on the arm. That simple, innocent touch sent a scorching heat through her veins. She pulled her arm away, and he jerked his hand back. Neither of them said a word for several seconds.

He was the one who broke the silence. "Hey, don't worry about me. The doc says I'll be fine. I just needed a couple stitches. I was lucky I didn't break anything."

"Yes, you were very lucky," Betty agreed, trying hard to keep her mind from being ruled by what had just happened. If she allowed herself to think about what she'd felt a few seconds ago, she'd never be able to work for this man and stay sane.

"Here we are," Mark said as he turned onto her street. "If you need a little time off, let me know, okay?"

"Time off?"

"You can count travel time as working hours."

"No, that's okay. I'll be at the office first thing in the morning."

"Dedicated, huh?"

"I guess you can say that."

As Mark drove away, Betty stared after his car from the porch. She unlocked the door, put her bag on the floor, then came back outside. Apparently, he hadn't seen her.

"How was it?"

Betty spun around to see Deanne right behind her. "We got the job done."

"Was Mark there the whole time with you?"

"No. Come on inside, and I'll tell you all about it."

Betty told Deanne every last detail. It sure was nice to have a girlfriend to share secrets with. Deanne was one person she could tell anything to, and never feel like she was being a complete idiot.

"Wow!" Deanne said when Betty was done. "Sounds intense."

"I really have to watch myself this time. I've never been attracted to a boss before."

Deanne let out a hearty chuckle. "Looks like you and I are in the same boat. What are we gonna do?"

"Well, for starters, we need to get some sleep. Tomorrow comes awful early when you have to get up for work."

"Hey, don't forget about tomorrow."

"Tomorrow?" Betty asked.

"Yeah, Steve wanted to show us the new shop he's thinking about buying."

Betty flinched as she tried to remember. "Did I miss something?"

"I might have forgotten to tell you. But you'll go, won't you?"

"Of course."

They lay in their beds and read for a couple hours, then Betty turned off the light on her nightstand. She fell asleep pretty quickly, but her dreams took over. She was hugging her pillow when her alarm went off the next morning.

Mark could hardly wait to get to the office. Ever since Betty had arrived, he'd found the old excitement over going to work—something he'd lost after he had to deal with Dunstan.

Betty was an incredible woman, but he knew he was treading on dangerous territory. Getting involved with a coworker could seriously backfire, which would put him at risk of losing everything he'd worked hard for. All he wanted was to have this job at the bank, which kept his dad from pestering him about moving up the corporate ladder, and plenty of time to surf.

He'd arrived an hour early this morning, and he'd positioned his chair so he could see when Betty arrived. The moment he spotted her, he pretended to be immersed in the paperwork in his folder.

Chapter Seven

"**G**ot any more training for me?" Betty asked from his door. He lifted his head and looked directly at her but didn't say anything right away. "Uh, good morning, Mark. How are you feeling?"

A slow grin crept over his face. "Better. Thanks for asking."

She remained standing there, waiting, feeling really awkward about how she'd barged in on him first thing. People walked behind Betty, and she stepped forward a little to let them by.

"Wanna come in and have a seat?" he finally asked.

"Sure." Should she close the door or leave it open? Betty hesitated for a few seconds before she decided to leave it open. She made her way to the chair closest to her.

"How do you feel about flying out of the nest today?"

"Wanna run that by me again?"

Mark leaned forward, and she saw the intensity on his face. Or was that pain from his surfing injury? The maternal instinct she seemed to have been born with kicked in, and it took all her self-control to hold back.

"When you first came here, I knew you had some experience, but I had no idea you were as knowledgeable and experienced as you are," he began. "But after I watched you in action, explaining the job to Nancy, I realized you could probably teach me a few things."

Betty felt a lump in her throat and her face grew hot. She nervously shifted her feet, crossing one ankle over the other then switching them. Mark smiled and waited. It was up to her to say something now.

"This is your call, Mark," she said.

"What do you want?"

She shrugged. "I want what's best for the bank."

He snickered and glanced away before returning her gaze. "You seem very committed to your career, so I'm going to let you decide if you need more training."

"If you feel that I'm ready to tackle the job without any more training, then I'd love to give it a shot."

There. She'd said it. Hopefully, he wouldn't feel that she was usurping his authority.

"Then let's give it a whirl. I have no doubt you can do the job if you really understand all you told Nancy."

Betty started to stand up, but Mark remained sitting. She wasn't sure what to do now, so she sank back into the chair. "This is the same basic thing I did back in Arizona, but I have a few more lines in my job description, right?"

"That's right," he agreed. "Which is why you got the promotion and increase in salary." Mark smiled, and for the first time in the office, he appeared relaxed.

She smiled back. She liked Mark when he was like this. Relaxed. Not waiting for something bad to happen. Then she remembered Harry Dunstan and what had caused his removal from his job.

"Of course, I'll give you regular reports on a daily basis, if that's what you want."

Mark pursed his lips and narrowed his eyes. Betty could tell he was deep in thought for a moment. Then he shook his head. "That really won't be necessary, Betty. I trust your judgment. You can turn in weekly reports and go over everything during our department meetings."

Betty nodded. "Is there anything else?"

He nodded as he stood. "There is." Betty felt herself tense as he came around from behind his desk and extended his hand. She slowly reached out and took it in hers. When their fingers touched for a handshake, she felt the tingle go up her arm, and she wanted to pull away, but she couldn't without being obvious. "Thanks." He relaxed his grip on her hand. "You were truly a big help in Hilo."

Now she was able to move. "You're welcome,

Mark. I really don't mind doing things like that since we're all supposed to be a team."

As Betty turned to leave, she felt him watching after her. All she wanted to do at the moment was make it to her office without tripping over her own feet. Mark had unnerved her, something that had absolutely never happened to her at work before. She needed to stay focused, or she was in a heap of trouble.

The first thing she did when she got to her desk was turn on her computer. Then she went straight to the program where she could build her schedule. It was still blank, since she didn't realize she'd be out of training so soon. She filled in several hourly slots with a basic agenda that she knew she'd need for the job.

Her next step was to check company E-mail, where she found new things to add to her schedule. Within a couple hours, Betty had her schedule for the next few days and the following week fairly full, leaving a few slots each day, in case she needed to do some shifting.

Betty had learned early in her career that organization was key to success in the banking business. She had to stick to a plan if she didn't want to feel overwhelmed, and it had worked well for her. She suspected it was the reason she'd been able to accomplish so much in such a short time. Each task had an allotted amount of time, and she knew when it was time to move on.

The day flew by, and it was time to go home. She'd gone to the break room to eat the sandwich she'd stuck in her purse when Deanne reminded her to bring something to munch on, just in case she didn't have time to go out to lunch. Thank goodness for Deanne.

When it was time to go home, Betty headed for the door, not paying much attention to where she was going, still thinking about the budget for a couple of the smaller departments in the bank. It was almost too late to stop when she almost ran right into Mark coming out of the elevator.

"Whoa," he said as he reached out to steady her. "Where's the fire?"

Betty laughed nervously. "I'm leaving for the day, if that's all right."

He raised his eyebrows and nodded. "Well, since you've been sitting at your desk all day without coming up for air, it's your prerogative to go home . . ." He glanced at his watch and looked back at her with amusement. "An hour after quitting time."

"I had a little catching up to do."

"Yes, but you don't have to do it all in one day. Dunstan took months to mess up the job, then the position was left vacant for another several weeks. Take your time, Betty. The bank's not going anywhere."

"But I like—"

"Order," he said, interrupting. "You're one of those people who thrives on everything being in its place and done on time, right?"

He knew her well. Sheepishly, she nodded. "I guess you have me figured out."

"Don't look so down. Being orderly is a good thing.

It seems to come naturally to you. I have to work at it."

Was Betty hearing correctly? Had Mark the office sourpuss just exposed a little of himself to her.

"You do?"

He sighed as he turned and started walking with her through the bank lobby. "I have a confession to make. I'm one of those guys who likes to roll out of bed around noon, hang out drinking coffee and reading the newspaper, then hitting the beach enough before dark so I can get some daylight surfing in. Then I can party all night."

And what a confession! Betty smiled back at him. "You sound a little like my brother."

"You have a brother? Where is he? Arizona?"

"He lives here, but he's on a business trip with his new wife."

"Interesting," he said. To Betty's surprise, he continued walking, even after she walked out of the bank. She'd expected him to say good night then turn back to his office. "I had no idea you had family here. What's up with that?"

Betty explained how her brother had gotten a scholarship to the University of Hawaii, and she'd followed him a few years later. He seemed genuinely interested in everything she had to say, which made her feel warm inside.

"Want a ride?" he asked, pointing to his Bug sitting by the curb. "I normally walk to work, but I wanted to go take a look at some surfboards on the North Shore right after work."

"I don't want to keep you."

"No problem," he said. He reached out and planted his hand in the small of her back, guiding her toward his car. "Your place is practically on the way. Unless, that is, you want to go with me."

"I'd love to, but I promised my roommate I'd go somewhere with her and her friend after work. As it is, I'll barely get home in time to change."

"We'll have to do it some other time, than," he said, his voice laced with disappointment.

They were at Betty's front door in five minutes. She hopped out, waved, and ran up the sidewalk to the front porch, where she glanced over her shoulder to see him still waiting. She waved again, and he waved back at her, then drove off. A deep breath escaped her lips as she felt the heaviness in her chest. No matter what she did to block her feelings, she found herself becoming more and more infatuated with Mark.

He'd been cold in the beginning, almost mean. He obviously hadn't trusted her. Even then, she saw a vulnerability in him that was a little disarming. But until he actually became nice and told her he had faith in her ability to do her job, she was able to fool herself into thinking she didn't feel anything for him.

There was still something about him, though, that gave her cause for worry. Mark seemed to have a restless spirit, almost as if he was waiting for something to happen. She'd watched him at work and during that afternoon they went to dinner on the Big Island. It was impossible not to notice how on edge he seemed.

Was it possible she was the cause of this? Maybe she made him nervous, but she couldn't imagine why. Betty considered herself an easy person to be around, and everyone else seemed to agree with her, including all the people she'd worked with back in Arizona. Why would things be any different with Mark.

Deanne was sitting on the sofa, her feet propped up on the coffee table, when Betty walked inside. "It's about time you got here. I thought you might not make it in time to go with us."

"Give me a minute to change, and I'll be ready."

"Okay, Steve will be here in five minutes."

Betty came out of the bedroom three minutes later, wearing bike shorts and an oversized T-shirt. Deanne shook her head. "You're amazing, Betty. You go from being a stuffy suit to looking like one of us in less than five minutes. I don't know how you do it."

"It's easy. I just toss all my business clothes on the bed and grab the first thing I find that looks comfortable."

Steve was right on time, pulling his van into their driveway and revving his engine. Deanne grabbed Betty's arm and said, "Let's not run out there. I don't want him to think I'm too eager."

"Come on, Deanne. You don't have to play games with Steve. Besides, he's your boss."

Deanne glanced down and then back up at Betty. "Yeah, I guess you're right. I better behave."

"Now don't go and do something like that. Behaving's no fun," Betty said, trying to lighten things up a bit.

Deanne laughed. "Don't I know it. Let's go."

"Hey, pretty ladies," Steve said as he looked adoringly at Deanne. Betty filed that in the back of her mind as she smiled. If Deanne ever doubted Steve in the future, Betty could remind her of his clear and open admiration. "Ready to go help me make the final decision?"

"Final decision?" Betty asked.

"I'm getting ready to move my shop. The beach rentals are doing great, but everything else is starting to slow down."

"Is there a reason for that?" Betty asked, her banker side showing through.

He chuckled. "Most likely because I'm starting to lose interest in it. I miss surfing, so I've been thinking about taking a partner and getting into a little teaching."

"Sounds like a great idea," Betty said. "It's always good to make changes, as long as they're well thought out."

"Believe me, I've been thinking about this for a very long time."

Deanne remained quiet as Steve spoke. Betty turned back to Steve. "So, why are we going along with you?"

"The new location is closer to the beach. It has a

room for a school and other water sports equipment, too, which might help me get a partner."

"Anyone in mind?" Betty asked.

Deanne looked at Steve. "Yeah, I was wondering the same thing. You keep talking about getting a partner, but you haven't mentioned any names."

Steve shrugged. "There is one guy, but he might be a hard one to convince."

"Never hurts to try."

"You're right," he said. "After I look over this shop one more time, I'm supposed to meet someone and show him some of my inventory I'm thinking about unloading to make room for new stock."

They hopped into Steve's van and got settled, Deanne in the front passenger seat, and Betty in the middle. Steve turned around and looked at Betty. "Did Deanne tell you I'm taking you ladies out to dinner tonight?"

"Sounds great," Betty said. She wasn't dressed for anyplace fancy, but then neither were Deanne and Steve.

It took them more than an hour to get to the shop Steve wanted to look at. He reached in his pocket, pulled out a key, and opened the door. "After you, ladies."

They all walked in and started sneezing. "When was the last time anyone swept this place?" Deanne asked as she blew on the dusty counter.

"Most likely two years ago, when there was a store

here. It's been vacant for a long time, which is why I'm getting such a deal on it."

Betty wandered around the shop, looking at all the space. She went from room to room, thinking how perfect it would be for Steve's new business—if he could bring it up to his high standards.

"It's gonna take quite a bit of work, but it looks good," Betty said.

Tilting his head forward, obviously pleased, Steve said, "Is that Betty the banker talking?"

"Yes, and the friend Betty, too. I really like it. Don't you, Deanne?"

"Uh, yeah, I like it." She reached out, ran her finger along a wall, then blew the dust off it. "Eww."

Steve laughed. "Looks like I'll have to find someone else to help me clean it."

"You got that right."

He showed them what his plans were for each area of the store. Betty was impressed by how much thought he'd put into it.

"If you need a loan, don't forget to start with First Guardian Bank," Betty said.

"Hopefully, I won't need a loan after I liquidate some of my dead inventory. But if I do, you'll be the first person I call."

"This is great, Steve," Betty finally said. "I think, with your experience in this business and your reputation, you can't go wrong."

Deanne nodded, glanced down at her feet, and added, "Okay, I'm hungry. Can we go eat now?"

Steve glanced at his watch and frowned. "I promised to meet friend over at the old shop. We're already a little late. That won't take long."

Deanne groaned. "I hope whoever it is doesn't talk a lot."

Betty smiled. She was hungry, too, but she'd momentarily forgotten about food. Steve's excitement and anticipation had rubbed off on her.

As they piled back into Steve's van, he turned to Betty. "Oh, I guess I better warn you. This guy we're meeting . . ." His voice trailed off, and he looked at Deanne, who appeared puzzled.

"What, Steve? What about the guy?"

"Betty knows him," he said, still looking at her.

Alarm bells went off in Betty's head. "I know him? From college?"

"Well, not exactly."

Deanne gave him a stern glare. "Out with it, Steve. Who are we meeting?"

"A guy by the name of Mark Diaz."

The alarm bells in Betty's head turned into screaming sirens. So Steve was the guy Mark was supposed to meet on the North Shore? Why hadn't she put two and two together?

Steve looked back apologetically. "I hope you're not mad."

"You set this up with Mark, didn't you?" Deanne said. Betty couldn't tell if Deanne was angry or just trying to sound that way.

"No, I promise, I didn't. Mark doesn't even know I'm bringing anyone."

"Are you sure?" Deanne's arms were folded over her chest, and she darted an amused glance back at Betty.

Whew! Deanne wasn't mad. She was just having a little fun.

Now all Betty had to worry about was her own reaction to what had just transpired. Was she ready to see Mark so soon after work? She glanced down at her bike shorts and wished she'd dressed a little nicer.

Chapter Eight

Deanne reached over and squeezed Betty's arm. "Are you okay with this?" Without waiting for a response, she turned to Steve. "Why didn't you say something, Steve? You know Mark is Betty's boss."

"I didn't think it mattered."

"Does Mark know I'm with you?" Betty asked.

"Not unless you told him."

Steve wouldn't look either Betty or Deanne in the eye. Betty turned to Deanne and saw that they both came to the same realization at the exact same time.

"Steve, you're matchmaking!" Deanne said.

He rolled his eyes. "I'd never do anything so low. How can you say that?"

Deanne growled. "Men!"

They were almost at the shop, and Betty's knees felt weak. Maybe she'd stay in the van while Steve conducted business with his old friend. He didn't need her for what he was doing.

Mark was standing, leaning against his car in the parking lot, waiting. He smiled when he spotted the van. He still hadn't seen her yet, and she wondered if, when he did, he'd still be smiling.

She quickly got her answer when Mark stuck his head in the side window as soon as Steve pulled into the lot. His smile faded only momentarily, then it broadened to twice the size. If she wasn't mistaken, it was real, too.

Holding up her hand and wiggling her fingers, Betty said, "Hi, Mark."

"Betty!" Turning to Steve, he looked puzzled. "How do you know her?"

Steve chuckled. "Betty and I go way back."

Mark's face turned crimson, then he stepped back. It was obvious what he was thinking. Fortunately, Steve put his mind at rest and saved Betty from having to explain.

"Deanne's her roommate, and I've been to their house several times."

"Oh," Mark said, apparently not convinced quite yet. His face lit up again. "Deanne's your roommate?" He turned and winked at Deanne. "What other secrets have you been keeping from me?"

Deanne leaned back and gave him a commanding look. "You'll never know. If we told you, they wouldn't be secrets."

Steve steered the conversation back to why they

were there. "I've got the boards in the back room. C'mon, Mark, let's go take a look."

By now, Betty realized that staying in the van didn't make sense, so she got out and followed them into the shop, which was still open. The young guy Steve had working for him had his chair leaning on the back two legs, reading a comic book.

"Dudes," he said as he lifted his glance then returned it to what had his interest before they'd arrived.

"Hey, Boogie," Steve said. "It's past closing time. You shoulda gone home an hour ago."

"Yeah, I know, but nothin's happenin' there. I figured I might as well stick around, just in case someone stops by, ya know."

Betty smiled at the twenty-something guy. She'd known plenty of guys like Boogie, who appeared to have no direction. Most of the time it was just arrested motivation that kicked in a little later than it did in most people. He'd probably be fine, after his parents realized he was too old to be living at home and decided to give him the heave-ho.

"Hey," Boogie said as he lifted a hand in an abbreviated wave. He put down the magazine and righted his chair. "This the guy you been tellin' me about, Steve?"

For a moment, Steve seemed a little flustered. He squirmed and made a crisp nod toward Boogie. "We'll talk about it later."

Deanne motioned for Steve to go on into the back room with Mark and stopped Betty before she followed them. Once the guys were out of the room, she whispered, "Yeah, he's the guy. Just don't say anything, okay?" She gave Boogie a pleading look.

Boogie held up his hands in apology. "All right, I don't want to mess anything up. I'm outa here. Be seein' ya."

Once he was gone, Betty turned to Deanne. "What was that all about?"

Deanne chewed on the inside of her cheek for a moment before she said, "Promise you won't tell a soul?"

"Of course."

"Steve's working on getting Mark into the business."

"What business?"

"Surfboards."

"Mark?" Betty couldn't imagine Mark doing anything but banking for a living.

"Steve's talked to several possible partners, but no one has Mark's business mind. Plus, he knows surfing better than anyone else we know."

"Do you think he'll do it?"

"Who knows?" Deanne said with a shrug.

"Has Steve said anything to him at all about the business, I mean?"

"Not yet. He's showing Mark the inventory and getting a feel for his level of interest."

"He's using psychology, huh? Not a bad idea." If Betty was completely honest, she'd done that in her past, too, and when she took the time to think things through, they almost always turned out great.

"Remember, Betty, you promised you wouldn't say a word."

Betty zipped her finger across her mouth. "Not a word."

The guys were in the back room for almost a half hour when Deanne decided they'd had enough time. "I'm so hungry, I'm ready to start gnawing on one of those boards."

"Me, too," Betty agreed.

"I guess I'll have to drag Steve out of there, or he'll never leave," Deanne said.

She was only gone for a minute before she came back with both Steve and Mark. Betty stayed in the front of the shop and pretended to be interested in the boards. Actually, some of them were pretty, but she wasn't about to use one.

"I guess we better leave," Steve said as he glanced at Deanne then back at Mark.

Disappointment clouded Mark's face, but he tried to hide it. Betty really enjoyed seeing him outside the bank, and she found herself hoping Steve would invite Mark to join them.

But he didn't. Instead, he told Mark to get back with him and let him know if he wanted any of the boards. And then he motioned for the women to follow him back to the van.

Once they were inside the van, Deanne said, "Why didn't you ask Mark to join us for dinner?"

Steve flashed a megawatt smile back at her. "It's not good to appear too eager."

"Who are you talking about?" Deanne asked, squinting her eyes at him. "Betty or you?"

"Me, of course. If Mark thinks it was his idea to go into business with me, he'll like it much better." With a sideways glance, he asked, "Why did you think I was talking about Betty?"

"Oh, you know exactly why. This was no accident, having them both at the shop at the same time."

Steve filled the van with his laughter. "That's one of the things I like about you, Deanne. You don't trust me."

"One of the things?" she said. "What's another?"

"You're a very smart woman."

Betty sat back and listened to this playful interchange and thought about what had just happened. Mark seemed to truly be in his element in a surf shop, but how could he manage to be part owner of this demanding business and still work in banking?

"Don't worry, Betty," Steve said as he grinned at her in the rearview mirror. "Mark won't know what hit him from either direction."

That was what worried Betty. He was getting hit from all sides, and she didn't want to stop it.

They stopped for dinner at a small seafood place halfway between the North Shore shop and Honolulu. Betty didn't say much; she mostly listened. Deanne and Steve argued over quite a few things, but Betty could tell it was all in fun. She admired the comfortable relationship they had, and she wondered if Deanne realized how relaxed she appeared around Steve.

After dinner, Steve took them home. Betty ran inside while Deanne lagged behind to say good night to Steve.

It was pretty late, so Betty decided to get ready for bed. She wanted to get an early start in the morning and get ahead a little at work. Betty hated working close to deadline, and the job had been vacant for so long, there were enough deadlines looming to stress her out and keep her up at night.

Mark arrived at the office at his usual time—an hour before everyone else was scheduled to report to work. But Betty was already there and had been there long enough to complete one task and get onto another.

"Well, good morning, sunshine," she heard from the doorway. Betty had been aware of him standing there watching, but she pretended not to notice.

She glanced up and smiled. "Hey, Mark. Buy any surfboards lately?"

To her dismay, her question elicited a frown. He shook his head and mumbled a few words then left.

Her heart sank. She'd obviously said something wrong, but she had no idea what. She went over and over the few words they'd exchanged, and she couldn't figure out how any of it would anger him.

Finally, after not being able to focus on her work, she got up, took a deep breath, then headed for Mark's office. He was standing in the corner, looking at something in his file cabinet. He turned and looked at her within a split second.

"Mark," Betty said tentatively, "may I come in?"

"Sure."

"I have no idea what I said that bothered you a few minutes ago, but I'm sorry for whatever it was."

He snorted. "You didn't say anything wrong. I just have a lot on my mind lately, and I acted like a jerk. I'm the one who should be apologizing."

Betty let out a sigh of relief. She never wanted to be a source of problems to her boss, no matter who it was.

"Anything you care to discuss?" she asked.

There was a brief silence before he shook his head. "No, I'll be okay. I just have to do quite a bit of serious thinking about some things. You're doing fine, Betty. Keep up the good work."

Mark felt awful about alarming Betty. She had no idea she'd said the word that triggered his anxiety. The very mention of the word "surfboard" set him on edge.

Although he'd advanced in banking with lightening speed, Mark wasn't sure he was suited to it, especially now. After looking at all Steve's excess inventory, ideas had floated through his mind, like possibly opening his own shop.

The way he saw it, that created two problems. For one thing, working full-time at the bank left him little time for anything else if he wanted to run a successful business. Secondly, he didn't want to compete with someone who'd been so kind to him and such a good friend. Steve was a man of high integrity, so there was no way he'd do anything to take business away.

Over the past few weeks, though, Steve had mentioned bits and pieces of his plans to expand, which was why he was getting rid of some of his old stock. He needed the capital to do the things that would take him to the next level. Mark had a little money saved, and he'd actually thought of asking Steve if he'd thought of taking on a partner.

But when would Mark find time to do any of the work? He couldn't very well hand Steve the cash and say, "Send me my share of the profit. Now I gotta go to work at the bank."

First Guardian Bank had been a great company to work for. He'd been given opportunities he never would have had anywhere else, due to his age when he started moving up. They never let age, gender, or race be an obstacle to anyone's career, and for the most part, it had paid off for the bank. Their profit was higher than anyone else's for their size.

Once, when Mark was a small child, he'd overheard his own father tell someone to follow his dreams, and he'd be successful. Should he heed that advice, knowing his father wouldn't consider the surfing business a serious endeavor?

All morning, he fumbled through files and tried to accomplish the impossible, keeping his mind on his work. Finally, he pushed back from his desk and figured it was time for lunch.

Mark walked past Betty's office and saw that the door was closed, and he didn't see that familiar light streaming from beneath the door. His heart sank. She'd already gone to lunch. He'd sort of hoped he might run into her, then he'd casually ask if she wanted to join him.

Oh well. He'd walk down to the beach, where he could get something from one of the snack wagons. He wasn't in the mood for a sit-down lunch, anyway. He was too restless.

Betty watched Mark leave the building. She'd joined Fran and a few other people from the office, and they'd gone to the cafe that catered to the business crowd.

Mark walked down the street, then crossed at the intersection and headed toward the beach. She lost sight of him a second later.

"Well, what do you think of that, Betty?" Fran asked.

"Huh?"

Fran leaned back and studied Betty. "You didn't hear a word we were saying, did you?"

"No, I guess not."

Snapping her fingers, Fran laughed and said, "Earth to Betty, come in, Betty."

"Sorry I'm not a better listener, Fran," Betty apologized. "It's hard for me to leave a desk piled so high with work that needed to get done yesterday."

"Man, you're really different from Mr. Dunstan. He

never missed lunch, and he took more than an hour everyday."

"Sounds like quite a guy," Betty said jokingly.

Rolling her eyes, Fran replied, "You can say that again."

When Betty returned to her desk, she flipped on her computer and checked E-mail. There were twenty-three messages since she'd left for lunch. After skimming them to see if anything was urgent, she clicked "save" and moved on to the next item on her list.

The day went by way too fast. She was nowhere near done with everything by the time everyone was heading out. Mark stopped at her office door.

"Such a workaholic," he said.

"Not really. There's so much catching up, I guess it could seem that way, but I'm very good at leaving when it's all done."

She fully expected him to leave, but he leaned against the door frame and folded his arms, watching her the whole time. Betty's hands began to shake as she typed the memo she'd been drafting.

"How much longer before you're done?"

"Days," she replied. "Maybe even weeks."

"You do realize the bank has a policy that you can't spend the night here."

Betty rested her elbow on her desk and looked at Mark. "No, I didn't realize that, but I guess it makes sense."

"Why don't you call it quits for tonight, and I'll drive you home?"

Her heart lurched. She knew the smart thing to do would be to turn him down, but she couldn't. Without allowing her conscience to talk her out of it, she pushed away from her desk. "Okay, sounds like a great idea. Let me get out of this program, and I'll be right with you."

He smiled, a look of surprise flashing through his eyes. To her delight, Mark seemed very happy that she'd accepted his ride.

Once they got in his car, Mark turned to her. "You know I want something in return for this ride, don't you?"

What could he possibly want from her? With a forced chuckle, Betty said, "How about letting me cook dinner for you one evening?" The minute those words left her mouth, she regretted it. What was she thinking?

Mark nodded. "Sounds like a fair exchange to me, but then I'd owe you something. Right now, I need something else from you."

"I'm all ears."

He shifted gears and pulled out into traffic. Betty stared at his face as he went through some sort of mental process that appeared to be anguish, but she wasn't sure and didn't want to jump to conclusions.

When he spoke, it was softly, and she had to lean toward him. "I've been thinking about doing something a little different with my life."

"Like what?"

"For as long as I can remember, I've had a desire that I never thought I could attain."

A desire. Was Mark asking her for advice in the romance department? Her heart fell, but she tried to keep a smile on her face.

"I'm sure that whatever you want is possible," she managed to say. "Maybe I can help you."

"There's this thing . . ." he began, pausing to look at her and smile. "Well, sort of a thing. Maybe more like a passion."

A passion. This was almost too much for her to bear.

"It's a passion I've been pursuing ever since I discovered it. I'm thinking about really going after this . . . passion, but for the first time in my life, I'm not certain." He snickered and shook his head. "I know I couldn't be any more vague, but I don't really know how to talk about it."

"Just tell me," Betty said.

"I really shouldn't, considering the position we're both in at the bank. Maybe I just need to do some serious soul-searching and figure things out on my own."

Betty knew she couldn't force him to talk. "Okay, if you change your mind, let me know."

He reached out and patted her hand. "You're a special woman, ya know that?"

She'd heard that before, or at least a variation of it. Betty the friend, the nurse, the confidant—she was all those things to a lot of people. Now she found herself wanting more.

The irony of her predicament wasn't lost on Betty. She had a very strict policy of never dating a guy from work. The time she'd spent with Mark hadn't been dates—although the kiss was still romantic—so she didn't want to count that. Now, Mark was confiding in her, obviously because he trusted her as a friend.

Betty only had one serious relationship at a time when she had to make a decision between her career and her relationship. She'd chosen her career, since she'd grown up with a mother who had always longed for a career of her own. Or at least that was what Betty thought at the time. After she'd returned home to Arizona, she learned that wasn't the case. Her mother had made the decision to do what she truly wanted to do—and that was to be a wife and mother. Sure, she'd wanted a career, but she wanted her family even more. As she wisely said, "Sometimes we have two excellent choices, so we can't lose either way."

Her mother's positive attitude had helped influence her decision to move back to Hawaii, the place where she felt at home from the moment she'd first set foot on the sand, inhaled the salty air, and heard her first ukulele.

They rode a few minutes in silence, until Betty decided to offer some standard advice. Hopefully it would cheer Mark up a little, even if it did mean she'd have to watch him pursue someone else.

"Mark, I can pretend to understand your passion,

but I do know that if you don't go after what you really want, it'll eat away at you until you're miserable."

He frowned. "That's exactly what's been happening, Betty. How did you know?"

She smiled at him, although she felt an empty spot in her chest. "Because I had a passion that I didn't act on right away, and it got so bad, I'd almost forgotten how to have fun."

Mark nodded, his attention focused on the road ahead. "I'm afraid that'll happen to me, too. It's not that I'm miserable in my current situation, because I'm not. But this passion, it's overwhelming. You know, like having an itch you can't reach to scratch?"

How well she knew. "Then you really need to act on it. Figure out how to do it, and then just dive in."

This time, Mark didn't pat her hand. Instead, he lifted his right arm and draped it over the back of her seat and touched her shoulder. Betty sat rigid, unsure of what to do.

When they got to her place, she started to get out, but Mark gently grabbed her by the arm. "Don't go in yet."

She sat back and nodded. "Still feel like talking?"

"Do I ever."

Betty noticed the curtain in the front picture window lift then fall back into place. Deanne was watching for her.

"Why don't we go inside, and I'll change?"

"Okay," he said. "If you don't mind, I'll grab my shorts out of the trunk and change, too."

Deanne was all smiles when they walked inside. "So," she said, "how's work?"

"Same old, same old," Mark answered before Betty had a chance. "Another day, another dollar."

"My, aren't we full of clichés?"

Betty showed Mark to the bathroom, and she went into the room she shared with Deanne. They both came out at the same time.

"Let's go somewhere," Mark said.

She hesitated then nodded. "Okay, fine."

"Going somewhere special?" Deanne asked when she saw them in shorts and T-shirts.

Mark turned to Betty. "Yeah, I thought I might take Betty out for something to eat, then a walk on the beach. Wanna go?"

"No," Deanne said slowly, smiling. "I think I'll just stay here and wait up for my roommate who really needs a break. Don't stay out too late."

Betty knew exactly what Deanne was saying. She didn't have much of a life, now that she was back in Hawaii, and Deanne was glad to see that was starting to change. Too bad Betty didn't have a chance to tell her about the conversation she and Mark had on the way here.

After carefully hanging his suit on the hook in the backseat, Mark got in and started his car. "Want seafood, steak, or chicken?"

"I don't care."

"Good. I'll pick." Mark drove to a place on the canal that specialized in both steak and seafood.

They were early enough to get seated right away. Service was fast and good, and Betty enjoyed the light chitchat with Mark through the meal. She waited for him to bring up his "passion," but he didn't during dinner. On their way out, he glanced over at the small boats for rent by the bridge.

The scene before her was breathtakingly beautiful. People strolled on the sidewalk along the Ala Wai Canal, while colorful boats puttered by, first a yellow boat, then a blue one.

"Wanna go for a boat ride?"

She smiled. "Sounds great."

"You're a great sport, Betty," Mark said. "You don't seem to mind trying a lot of different things. In fact, you seem like the type who'll do anything once."

"Oh, there are a few things I won't do," she replied with a chuckle.

"Like what?"

"Surfing for one."

"You've never tried it?"

She scrunched her nose. "Well, yeah, I tried it once, and I wiped out. You'll never get me back on another surfboard."

He playfully pointed a finger at her. "But at least you tried it. My assessment still stands."

Chapter Nine

They approached the boat rental stand to see a smiling young Hawaiian woman. "What color boat would you like, sir?" she asked Mark directly.

He turned to Betty then looked back at the woman. "Blue."

Betty felt a little put off that he hadn't even bothered to see if she preferred a color, but she didn't say anything. As they were stepping down into it, he steadied her by holding her hand. He offered her the wheel. "In case you were wondering, I chose blue because it looks so good on you. When I looked down and saw the royal blue boats, there was no doubt in my mind what color we should be in."

He'd just redeemed himself in her eyes. She smiled at him without saying a word. She had no clue what to say.

Betty had maneuvered the boat away from the dock before Mark started talking again. "Now that I've got you out over the water, I wanted to tell you something."

"What's that?"

"You're doing a great job at the bank. I'm pretty embarrassed about how I treated you in the beginning. Sorry I acted like such an idiot."

Not knowing what else to do or say, Betty laughed. "You weren't acting like an idiot. You were just doing your job."

"No, I should have paid closer attention to your credentials. I have a confession to make."

"Go ahead." Betty had pretty good control of the boat, and she was comfortable moving along at a slow pace, cruising the canal.

"I never even looked at your personnel records until after your first day in the Honolulu branch." He folded his arms over his chest and stretched out his legs. "You're probably more qualified than I am for my position."

"I wouldn't say that." Betty felt embarrassed and didn't know what to say to such flattery.

"Really. When they told me to rewrite the training manual for a trial run, I figured you'd be the first student. Man, did I have egg on my face."

"Who told you to rewrite the training manual?"

"The regional manager. He said we needed everything spelled out in black and white to keep what happened with Dunstan from happening again."

"So that's why you had me jumping through hoops."

"Yeah, that's why. What had me confused in the beginning was how quickly you breezed through the material, while Nancy was floundering and not catching on."

"How much experience did Nancy have before moving into her position?"

Mark shook his head. "Very little in banking. She was in retail for several years before making the move. First Guardian started her in the Consumer Loans department, then moved her to operations."

"That's the difference, right there," Betty said. "I've been in operations since I started with the bank. I had that training, even though it was from the old handbook. Most of what I learned came from practical experience."

"At least I understand that now. Nancy's a very smart woman. I'm glad you were able to explain to her what I botched in the training manual."

"You didn't botch it," Betty said, fearing she was walking on eggshells here. She needed to be careful how she phrased things. Forgetting she was with her boss could be a fatal error to her career. "There are a few rough spots that are slightly confusing, but a tweak here and a few extra explanations there will take care of it."

"Would you mind giving me a hand with that next week?" Mark looked at Betty in such a way that she couldn't possibly turn him down, even though she already had a full schedule.

"That's fine. I'll do whatever I can to help out. We're a team, right?"

Mark smiled and nodded as he let out a long sigh. Then he sat up a little straighter as he nodded toward the boat's steering wheel. "Want me to take over? I've bent your ear about work enough, and I'm sure you could use a break."

Betty tilted her head back and laughed. "Whatsamatter, Mark? Afraid of my driving?"

He folded his arms again and shook his head. "No, not at all. In fact, I'm enjoying being a passenger. Sometimes I get tired of being in control."

Betty cast a quick sideways glance at Mark then focused back on where they were going. That last comment of his was pretty powerful, and she wondered how deeply he meant it. At the office, he definitely came across as a control freak, but now, he was relaxed and actually fun.

Even beyond that, something about Mark was different. She'd noticed it ever since he'd looked at Steve's excess inventory.

A few days after they met, she knew he was different at work from how he was outside of the office. At the bank, he still wore a stone face—at least when he wasn't talking to her. But when he left work, he was relaxed, talkative, and quite fun. This was something she could get used to, but she knew she'd better not allow herself to enjoy it too much.

The comments he'd made right after work about his "passion" kept floating through her mind, bringing her back to reality. No matter how much fun she was having with Mark at the moment, she had to keep a couple of very important things in mind. First, he was her boss, which was forbidden territory in the romance department. Second, he had a passion for someone else, meaning he was using her for a sounding board, a buddy. Good old Betty, best friend to all, someone to lean on. She sighed. That was the story of her life, so she might as well accept it.

"Ready to head back?" he said after they puttered along in silence for several minutes.

"Sure." Betty carefully turned the steering wheel and had the boat going back in the direction of the rental dock.

Once she parked the boat, he hopped out, then offered her a hand, gently lifting her as if she were weightless. She pulled her lips between her teeth to keep from gasping at how good his touch felt.

Mark took hold of her hand as they walked back to his car as if it were the most natural thing in the world. Betty knew she should have avoided all physical contact with him, but she didn't want to. To the contrary, she wanted to grab hold of him and pull him even closer. But she didn't. She just accepted his gesture of friendship and told herself to accept things at face value rather than try to read between the lines or force anything he didn't want.

He helped her into his car, then went around to the

driver's seat. "You don't seem to mind riding around in my little Bug."

"I don't," she replied. "This is more than I have."

Mark slapped himself on the forehead. "Oh, yeah, I almost forgot. I need to call my friend about finding you a car."

"No hurry."

He set his jaw as he looked in the rearview mirror before backing out. "I said I'd do it, and I will. I never make promises I can't keep."

What an admirable trait. Betty wanted to let him off the hook, but as adamant as he was about helping her find a car, she knew it was futile to even try.

Betty was surprised when they pulled up in front of the house and he hopped out to walk her to the door. She'd expected him to drop her off and pull away.

"Thanks, Betty," he said as they stood on the porch. She glanced over to see if Deanne was watching, but there was no sign of her. "You've been a big help. I don't know what I would have done without your listening ear."

"That's quite all right, Mark. What are friends for?"

He appeared confused for a split second, but he quickly recovered. "Yeah," he agreed. "What are friends for?"

After Betty went inside, she was relieved to be home alone. Obviously, Deanne hadn't waited for her at home. Betty's mind was racing with events of the day, and she didn't feel like discussing anything right now.

Fortunately, Deanne didn't return home until much later that night. Betty had just turned off the bedroom lamp and rolled over to her side, her back facing the door. Deanne tiptoed around the room, being very quiet, but Betty knew she was there.

Betty was right, Mark thought as he pulled up in front of his house and got out. If he didn't pursue his passion, surfing, he may never be totally satisfied. So what if he turned out to be a big disappointment to his dad. He'd already tried things his father's way, and he wasn't happy. Granted, he wasn't completely miserable. In fact, he was actually pretty satisfied and could coast most of the time, especially when things were going right. But the incident with Dunstan had blindsided him and made him regret ever taking that job with the bank.

Then along came Betty, the most intelligent woman Mark had ever met. She was pretty, but that seemed minor next to all her other remarkable qualities. She was a competent operations manager, freeing him up to oversee all of the Hawaii bank branch operations. He had more free time to surf now, not being forced to do his job and the operations manager's job, too. On top of everything else, she'd done most of Nancy's training, showing him that if he were to ever leave the bank, there would be someone to step into his shoes.

Steve had been more than obvious about his motives the other night when he'd called and offered all his excess inventory. He'd assured Mark that all he wanted to do was unload some surfboards, but then he'd gone into a long dissertation about how great the surfing business is and how it was time to expand if he could only find a partner.

Mark had been thinking about going into business on his own. A partnership would never work for someone like him, unless he was paired with someone who was open to new ideas. He'd known Steve for years. In fact, Steve's surfboard rental shack on Waikiki was the only place Mark would ever send a corporate executive from the mainland. He knew they'd be treated fairly and even offered a discount if they mentioned they were from First Guardian Bank and Mark had sent them.

With his passion for surfing, his mind for profit, and his understanding of business, Mark was pretty sure he'd be successful, whether he joined Steve in partnership or struck out on his own. The problem with having his own surf shop was that he'd be competing with a friend. Partnering with Steve solved one major problem right there.

He had so much on his mind, he knew he'd never be able to go to sleep right away. So he went out to his surfboard storage area and pulled a couple out and hoisted them up on the makeshift waxing rack he'd built. Nothing relaxed him more than feeling the texture of his favorite boards.

Mark worked himself into exhaustion. Finally, he put the boards away and went inside, nearly collapsing into bed. Sleep came quickly.

Morning came too quickly. For the first time since he'd started working at the bank, Mark barely made it to work on time. As expected, Betty was sitting at her desk, fully engrossed in the project she was currently breezing through.

He studied her for several seconds, hoping she wouldn't look up and he could get a better look at the most remarkable woman he'd ever met. Her shoulder-length, honey-colored hair with sun-kissed streaks glistened in the morning sunlight that shone through her office window. He loved the way she looked.

Suddenly, she glanced up and smiled, illuminating the entire room. "Good morning, Mark. Oversleep?"

Trying to act nonchalant, he shrugged. "Sort of. I couldn't go to sleep last night."

She frowned, her concern for him warming his heart. "Did I say something that bothered you?"

"Oh, no, it wasn't anything you said. In fact, if anything, you helped me."

Her face visibly relaxed. "If I ever say or do anything that keeps you up late at night, please tell me, okay?"

"You'll be the first to know."

Mark went into his own office and closed the door. He didn't feel like facing anyone yet, at least not until he had a chance to get his mind back into First Guardian Bank mode.

Fran walked into Betty's office with a cup of freshly brewed coffee. "I hope this is how you like it."

Betty smiled up at her secretary. "You don't have to bring me coffee, Fran. I can get it myself."

Nodding toward the steaming cup, Fran said, "You brought my coffee last time, now taste that and let me know if I got it right."

"Yes, ma'am." With a mock salute, Betty lifted the mug to her lips and tasted it. "Perfect. Thanks."

"So, are you enjoying your job here yet?" Fran asked, not making any moves toward the door.

Betty bobbed her head in a half nod. "Yes, so far, it seems to be going well."

"I noticed Mr. Diaz hasn't been on your case as much about the training manual he wrote. That's good, huh?"

With a chuckle, Betty replied, "I suppose that's good. The manual is pretty important, though, so I think I might help him fine-tune it."

Fran rolled her eyes. "I should hope so. You wouldn't believe how many times Nancy from Hilo used to call with questions. She had to talk to Mark at least two or three times a day." She sighed. "But he didn't seem to mind, if you know what I mean." She lifted her eyebrows and wiggled them suggestively.

"Really?" Betty stopped trying to pretend to work and looked up at Fran. "What, exactly do you mean?"

"Well, Nancy isn't exactly a dog, and Mr. Diaz is single, ya know."

Either Fran was gossiping about someone she knew nothing about, or she was on to something. Could

Nancy possibly be the passion Mark had been talking about?

"Nancy is married," Betty said.

"She is?" Fran seemed genuinely surprised. "I had no idea."

"When I went to the Big Island, she talked about getting home to her husband."

"I've been meaning to ask you," Fran said more casually than Betty was comfortable with, "how was her training?"

"She caught on pretty fast," Betty said, feeling defensive toward Nancy and wishing she hadn't opened the door for Fran's gossip. "Have you heard from her lately?"

"Only once, but that was when she called Mark and his secretary was out to lunch. We cover phones for each other."

"Did she have a question about the training manual?" Betty asked, wishing she could just mind her own business, but it was too hard. She was dying to hear the answer.

"I'm not sure. She must have said something pretty funny because I heard Mr. Diaz laughing his head off."

Betty swallowed hard. "I'll call her later and see if she has any questions."

Fran took that as her cue to leave. "I guess it's time to get back to work. We can chat later."

After Fran left, Betty rubbed her forehead. She didn't know what she'd said or done to encourage

Fran's instant familiarity, but she needed to keep things on a more professional level around the office. Being the subject of office gossip wasn't good, and Betty knew that Fran was free with her opinions about everyone in the office.

The day seemed to drag after that, so when it was quitting time, Betty was ready and out the door. Mark was nowhere in sight, Betty realized as she looked around the lobby. She'd halfway expected to see him waiting for her and possibly even offer a ride home.

She laughed out loud at herself as she began walking toward the bus stop. This was absolutely ridiculous. Mark had been generous with rides a couple of times, but she should never expect anything from him.

To her surprise, Deanne was home, watching television, when she arrived. "I thought you had to work this afternoon."

"Steve sent me home. He said I needed a little time off before next semester." She didn't sound happy about being given a break.

"I agree. My last semester of college was the hardest for me because I couldn't wait to finish." Betty sighed. "And now I find myself wishing I was back in school. Things were so simple then, and I had all my hopes and dreams for the future."

Deanne stared at her for a few seconds then looked back at the TV without saying anything. Betty wondered what she was thinking but didn't ask.

After changing clothes, Betty joined Deanne. "Whatcha watching?"

"Some scandalous talk show. These people are pathetic, aren't they?"

Betty looked up and saw mothers and daughters screaming at each other and nodded. "I wonder if all that's staged. I can't imagine talking to my mother like that."

"I just wish I had a mother," Deanne said, her voice cracking.

Deanne's mother had died right after she'd started college, which had made her first year very difficult, since she didn't have anyone to share the usual moving-away-from-home problems with. While other young women were calling home, Deanne had to figure things out on her own. Betty knew this was one of the reasons the two of them had hit it off so well— Betty had taken some of her own mother's advice and passed it on to Deanne. And when Betty's parents visited, they always invited Deanne to join them for dinner out and shopping trips.

Finally, Deanne flipped the TV off and announced, "I can't take it anymore. Let's go for a walk."

In the short time since Betty had been back, she realized they'd fallen into a routine, which was comforting. However, she also knew things would change. First of all, their two housemates would be returning soon, and secondly, something had to give between Deanne and Steve. Deanne wasn't the type to worry about a guy for too long before she moved on and found someone new.

They took their usual route, headed straight for the

beach. Betty had missed the sounds and smells of the ocean when she'd moved back to Arizona, although there were things she liked about being home. For one thing, her mother was a pretty wise woman, and she generally knew what to do at times like this.

"You like him quite a bit, don't you?" Deanne said, breaking the silence between them.

"Yes, very much." Betty decided it was best to not play games and pretend she didn't know what Deanne was talking about.

"But you don't want to get involved with your boss."

"Exactly."

Deanne sighed. "Maybe Steve will talk him into going into business and your problem will be solved."

Betty smiled at her friend's attempt to cheer her up. "That would be nice, but there are no guarantees that he'll feel any differently about me if he's not my boss."

"Oh, he won't feel differently," Deanne assured her. "I can see his attraction to you. It's so obvious."

"That doesn't solve your problem, though, does it?" Betty asked. "Steve is still your boss, and you don't want to take a chance and ruin that relationship."

They both stopped short when they looked up and spotted the men they were discussing, both of them wearing surfing shorts, inspecting surfboards, and deep in conversation. Betty stretched out her arm and backed Deanne up a few steps.

"What now?" Deanne asked.

"I don't know what to do."

"Let's go in another direction. Maybe we can sneak back to the sidewalk and go up a few blocks. Think they saw us?"

Betty shook her head. "I'm pretty sure they didn't."

Steve glanced over his shoulder to see what Mark was staring at. "Think that's the girls?"

"I'm pretty sure it is."

"I wonder where they're going," Steve said. "Wanna go check it out?"

Mark thought for a second, then shook his head. "Nah, I don't think so."

"Then how 'bout it, Mark? Wanna quit working at the bank and join me? I've already got a great business going. All I need now is someone with a mind for numbers crunching and a love of surfing."

Mark tilted his head forward and lifted his eyebrows. "And some extra cash that I just happen to have sitting around waiting for the right investment opportunity, right?"

Steve smiled as he shrugged. "Yeah, well, there is that."

"It's tempting, man."

"Then just do it. You only live once."

Mark glided his hands over the smooth texture of the surfboard and felt the tug to follow his heart. "I still need to think about it."

"Sounds like that's all you've been thinking about lately."

"You just told me that's what you've been working on," Mark said.

"And you had me figured out the whole time, too."

"The whole scheme was pretty obvious."

"Want some advice, Mark?" Steve said.

Mark shrugged but didn't respond. He knew Steve would offer advice whether he wanted it or not.

"You have to do this to prove to yourself that you've got it in you."

If only Mark could prove to his family this was a worthwhile business. "There are other things, too."

"Betty?"

"What about Betty?"

"I see you lookin' at her. You got it bad."

Mark belted out a chuckle. "Am I that obvious?"

"Oh, yeah."

"She's one smart woman, and she seems to know where she's going in life."

"That's not all bad."

"No," Mark agreed. "In fact it's good. For her."

"Don't tell me she intimidates you."

"Of course not. I'm not intimidated by anyone."

Steve turned his head as if looking to see if the women had returned. "I didn't think you were."

One thing Mark knew was that if he remained at the bank, he needed to keep his relationship with Betty on a professional and friendship level, especially since she worked directly beneath him. But if he went into business with Steve, there would be no stopping him.

He could pursue her and things could happen naturally.

"Let me think about this some more, and I'll get back to you, okay, Steve?"

"Sure thing. I'm not asking anyone else, so there's no rush."

Mark liked that about Steve. No rush, no pressure, no games, just an open and honest offer.

"Hey, Steve, wanna go see if that was Betty and Deanne we saw and not some mirage?"

Chapter Ten

"Think they saw us?" Betty asked.

"I don't think so, but maybe. Steve's pretty sharp."

"Oh well." They'd walked a few blocks away and used an open-air hotel lobby to cut through to the beach, where they were now sinking their toes in the sand.

"How's the job?"

"Different from Arizona."

"Like it? Be honest."

Betty snorted. "Honestly? I'm not sure what to think yet. It's basically the same position with a few more responsibilities thrown in. People here do business differently, though, and no one's in any hurry."

"I thought that's what you missed."

In her personal life, yes, but Betty was used to making things happen quickly at the office, showing off her talent in banking. She knew that was the reason she'd managed to make the move to where she was without any trouble.

They walked about a hundred yards before Betty spoke. She knew Deanne was waiting for a response.

"I love Hawaii, and I wouldn't want to change a thing about it."

"At least you can come to the beach to relax after work. What did you do in Arizona?"

"Most of the time, I just sat in my apartment, exhausted. After dinner, I went to a health club to work out, but then I always came straight home and went to bed early." That had only been weeks ago, but it seemed longer than that.

"Sounds pretty boring."

"It was. But Arizona's nice if you have a family. All my friends from the office had their kids' softball and soccer games to look forward to."

"You dated, didn't you?"

"Yeah, but nothing serious. Deep down, I think I always knew I'd come back here, so I didn't let a relationship develop."

"I'm so glad you knew that," Deanne said with sincerity. "Things haven't been the same without you here."

"Calmer, I suspect."

"Sort of. But then we had the excitement of Leilani with Jeff."

"Speaking of Leilani and Jeff, they're due back soon."

"I know. I can't wait."

Betty's mind took a sharp turn at the reminder of her brother and new sister-in-law. "Why don't we plan a party for them?"

"Great idea! A welcome home party!"

"I've got keys to their place. We can surprise them when they arrive."

Deanne frowned. "I don't know. Will that be okay with them?"

"Probably. If not, I know my brother well enough that he'll pretend it's okay, then give me grief about it later, but who cares. It'll be fun. Let's do it."

The remainder of the walk was spent talking about the party they were now going to have for Leilani and Jeff. Betty was thankful not to have to discuss her feelings for Mark anymore.

"Should we invite Steve and Mark?" Deanne asked.

"Steve, yes, but I'm not sure about Mark. Lani and Jeff don't know him."

"It'll be a great time for them to get to know him."

"I don't know," Betty said.

"If you don't invite him, I will," Deanne announced. "You can't get off that easy. I know you're putting off introducing your brother to the guy you're crazy about."

"He *is* my boss, remember?"

"And I'm sure Jeff will approve."

"I don't think you heard what I just said."

Deanne turned and grinned. "Look alive," she said as she nodded her head toward the beach.

When Betty turned her attention in the direction of Deanne's nod, she saw two very gorgeous men sauntering toward them, both of them focused and determined. Steve ran the last twenty feet, while Mark actually slowed down, never taking his eyes off her. Betty's heart thudded hard in her chest.

"Hey, why didn't you stop and chat?" Steve asked Deanne. "You ran away the minute we saw you."

Deanne glanced at Betty and grinned. "We had a few things to discuss."

"Like what?" Steve asked, putting his fists on his hips.

Tilting her head to one side, she actually batted her eyelashes, to Betty's surprise. "Like a party," she replied.

"Are we invited, or is this a girl thing?"

Betty stepped up. "It's for my brother and Lani."

Steve turned to Mark to explain. "Newlyweds."

"Oh," Mark said as he took a step back.

Betty couldn't help but notice how he'd shied away from the topic of newlyweds. Maybe he had a problem with romance.

Her mind reeled with the possibility of that as Deanne told Steve what they'd planned for Jeff's and Lani's homecoming. He invited himself and said he'd bring Mark and some munchies. Several minutes later, the guys turned back to what they were doing, and Deanne and Betty were on their way home.

"Did you see Mark's face?" Deanne asked. "That guy looked like he'd seen a ghost."

"Was that what it was? I noticed he got awfully quiet."

"The minute we mentioned having a party for your brother, he clammed up."

"I thought it had more to do with the fact that my brother is a newlywed."

Deanne's head snapped around. Her eyebrows were knit with confusion. "Who knows what the problem was? Maybe you'll find out tomorrow."

"I seriously doubt it," Betty said. "We don't talk much at work. There's too much to do."

"I can't imagine Mark working at a bank. I know he must be pretty good at it because he's pretty high up, but he's so laid-back."

With a snicker, Betty shook her head. "He's not laid-back at the office. People stand at attention when they know he's coming down the hall."

"That's a side I just can't see."

"He definitely has two sides, and they're different as night and day," Betty said. "When I first met him, I never would have imagined him being a surfer."

"Funny how people can fool you, isn't it?" Deanne said.

"Very funny."

Neither of them said another word until they reached home. Deanne unlocked the front door, then they both went inside and turned on just enough lights to see since it was starting to get dark.

"Oh, before I forget," Deanne said as she moved through the house. "We're gonna have to put off going to Sandy beach. Steve has me scheduled to work Saturday."

"Don't worry about it," Betty said. She really wasn't in the mood to go to the beach tomorrow, anyway.

Smiling, Deanne said, "Maybe you can talk Mark into taking you instead."

Betty chose not to respond to that. "I think I'll stay up and read a while," she said as Deanne headed for the bedroom.

She sat and stared at the page of her book for several minutes before even attempting to read a word. This was the first time she'd seen Mark serious outside the bank. Before, he was always smiling and showing her a side she felt showed the real Mark. Now she wondered.

After nearly an hour of trying to concentrate on her book, Betty finally gave up and went to bed. Deanne was already asleep, which was good. Betty didn't feel like talking.

The next couple of days, Mark was in Hilo, so Betty was able to work without thinking he might pop into her office at any minute. She got more work done than she had scheduled, which Mark was thrilled about when he returned on Friday morning.

"We're ahead of schedule," he said, his face showing no sign of stress. "Let's celebrate."

Something had happened to Mark in Hilo. He was different. "Okay, what do you suggest?"

"We can go out on the town tonight, then tomorrow I'll take you looking for a car."

Betty knew she should tell him she couldn't go with him, but her desire to be with Mark—especially when he was in this kind of mood—overtook her business sense. "Sounds great."

"I'm leaving early, but I'll pick you up at eight. We can go to a comedy show if you like that sort of thing. Or we can dance."

It had been a long time since Betty had seen a comedy show, so she said, "I need to laugh. Let's go to the comedy show."

"Sounds good to me, too."

Betty couldn't remember when she'd had so much fun in her life. As they left the club, Mark took her hand, and they walked along Kalakaua Avenue, looking at people and talking about how funny the comedian was. That night, when he took her home, he said, "Betty, you're a very special woman." She waited for him to say something else, but he didn't right away.

"I had a lot of fun, Mark. Thanks for everything."

"Can you be ready at ten in the morning? My friend said he has several cars you might like."

"Sure," she said as she reached over to get out.

"Wait a minute. I want to walk you to your door."

Betty smiled at how sweet Mark was being. He gently placed his hand in the small of her back and guided her up the sidewalk. When they reached the porch, he turned her around and clasped his hands behind her neck. "Tonight was special for me, Betty."

"Me, too."

Betty wasn't sure what was going to happen next, until his face closed in on hers for another kiss. Only this time, it was short and very sweet.

He backed up a step and touched her nose with the tip of his index finger. "See you in the morning, Betty."

"How was the date?" Deanne asked the second Betty let herself in.

"I think it was great, but I'm not sure." And that was the truth.

"Men!"

Betty laughed at Deanne's one-word exclamation. "I agree."

The knock came at the door at precisely ten o'clock the next morning. Betty was ready and waiting.

All morning, she test drove cars and became more confused with each automobile. Finally, Mark turned to his friend and said, "She'll have to think about it. I'll call you later and let you know."

This time, when Mark walked her to her door, he didn't even stop to kiss her. Instead, he turned her toward him and said, "Betty, I've never felt this way about a woman before. This is very awkward, too, since we work together."

"Yeah," Betty agreed. "Maybe we better not see each other anymore."

He suddenly looked stricken. "You really feel that way?"

Betty felt sick to her stomach as she nodded. "Yes, I'm afraid so."

The rest of the weekend was really lousy. Betty moped around the house for the remainder of Saturday, and she stayed in bed until noon on Sunday. Deanne made her get up for their walk to the beach. Betty was relieved when she didn't see Mark. She figured since it was a weekend, he must have gone to the North Shore for some serious surfing.

On Monday, Mark was at the office when she first arrived. She stopped by his office and smiled. He glanced up from his computer monitor and offered a crisp nod. Taken aback but not completely surprised by his instant return to formality, she scurried to her own office.

Fran came in a half hour later. "I'm early," she announced. "Proud of me?"

"Yes," Betty replied. "Very proud."

"What's up with Mark? You two have a fight?"

"A fight? Heavens no. What gives you that idea?"

With a shrug, Fran replied, "After your trip to Hilo with him, he's been rather nice. I figured you were either going out or just hanging out, and you were showing him a good time."

Betty squirmed. "We're friends." Or at least they *were* friends before last night.

"Oh well, we were hoping."

"We?"

Fran giggled. "Some people in the office were sort of speculating, if you know what I mean."

The people in this office sure did speculate about Mark a lot, first with Nancy and now with Betty. They needed to stop that.

"Mark wouldn't do anything to risk his professionalism," Betty said in his defense. "He's been a very good boss, and he wanted to make sure Nancy and I both caught on to our jobs." Betty's tone was rather harsh, but she needed to make sure her secretary got the point.

"Oh," Fran said, her eyes wide and her face turning bright red. "Sorry."

"Don't worry about it. But I'd really appreciate it if you wouldn't talk about anything inappropriate in the office, Fran."

"Okay." Fran was out of sight in a matter of seconds.

Betty felt awful that she had to do that, but Fran had stepped over the line several times. The last thing she needed was for her career to be messed up by an office love scandal—especially one that didn't exist.

There was a department head meeting planned for late morning, so Betty quickly gathered everything she thought she'd need. She hopped up from her desk and was almost out the door when she saw Mark round the corner. Okay, take two deep breaths and proceed, she told herself. He's just another person who works here. A man. Her boss.

To Betty's surprise, Mark had saved her a seat. Two long tables had been brought into the meeting room and shoved together to form a big square table that provided enough space for all the managers to sit and take notes. Mark was positioned in the center of the one facing the window.

She'd sought him out then felt her face grow hot when his gaze met hers. Instead of glancing away, he motioned for her to join him. After a split second hesitation, she smiled and walked around the room to where he was holding her spot.

"How many people come to these things?" she whispered.

"Oh, about twenty."

"I'm ready," Betty told him. "Want me to give the report?"

He looked surprised. "You want to do the report already?"

"Yeah, why not?"

"I don't know, I just thought . . ." His voice trailed off as he stumbled over his words. "Never mind. I'll be more than happy to let you give the report. You'll do fine."

Betty had never questioned whether or not she'd do fine. She knew she would. In fact, she'd given more than her share of reports in meetings just like this one, and she'd even conducted several of the meetings. She felt her pride taking over as she thumbed through her notes to keep from saying something she'd later regret. Handsome or not, Mark Diaz was still her boss. In his off hours, he was a happy-go-lucky surfer, but on company time, he was still a sourpuss, and she better not ever forget that.

During the first part of the meeting, Betty began to wonder why Mark had saved her a spot. But when he was asked to say a few words, he introduced her and said, "This is my new branch operations manager here in Honolulu. She's coming along very nicely with the training program I've put together."

Suddenly, Betty felt tongue-tied. Coming along *nicely*? With the training program *he* put together? She wanted to reach out and toss that pitcher of ice water over his head. But of course, she didn't. Instead, she smiled like the good employee she was.

Betty now knew exactly what she was dealing with. Mark was an opportunist, something she hadn't seen in a very long time. He was the crafty type, too. He'd pretended to accept her competence and even complimented her on accomplishing something he hadn't been able to do through his training program.

When it was Betty's turn to give her report, she found herself stuttering and fumbling through all the details. There was a brief hesitation before everyone clapped. She was greeted with a "Welcome, Betty" and "Great to have you on board" from the more outgoing people in the group. By the time she sat down, she wanted to crawl beneath the table, and bite her boss on the ankle.

Mark reached over and patted her on the hand. "Good job, Betty. It'll get easier with experience."

She yanked her hand away and looked in the opposite direction, pretending to be listening to the next department head report. All the while, she was seething inside and imagining all the ways she could inflict torture on the man seated next to her.

Once the meeting was over, Mark said, "Oh, I forgot to tell you, after the meetings, we like to go down to Perry's Smorgasbord for lunch."

"Oh, really?" Betty said sarcastically as all sorts of comments sprang to her mind.

However, a woman from the accounting department made her way over and grabbed Betty by the arm and started talking a mile a minute.

"I heard about all your success in Arizona, Betty, and I'm so glad to have you with us. You'll be such an asset to the Honolulu branch."

"Yes, well—" Betty began before Mark interrupted her.

"Hey, I don't want to take all your time, Betty. Mix and mingle, get to know everyone else," he said as if it were his idea.

She was fuming as he walked away. But she forced herself to smile at the woman who'd resumed her monologue about all the magnificent things she'd heard from the people in Arizona. Fortunately, Betty didn't have a chance to get a word in edgewise.

As Mark had said, the entire group went to Perry's, and Betty went with them. She could feel Mark's gaze, but she didn't look him in the eye. He'd crossed the line this morning, and she wasn't about to let him off the hook.

When they got back to the bank, she made a beeline

for her office and closed the door. There was work to be done, and it wouldn't take much to distract her.

Mark knew Betty was mad at him, but he had no idea why. He'd complimented her to the entire management team of the bank, saying how well she was doing. While at Perry's, he'd thought he might wait until they were back from lunch and discuss it with her, but she'd practically slammed her office door in his face.

No matter which of his tricks he used to concentrate on his work in front of him, Mark wasn't able to focus on banking business all afternoon. Too many things ran through his mind. He'd been toying with the idea of taking Steve up on his business offer and trying to figure out a way to let his parents know without starting a family war. Surfing was what he loved more than anything, and he knew Steve's business was profitable. After Steve had shown him the books, he was pleasantly surprised at just how well the surfing business actually was doing. With the expansion, both Mark and Steve would be able to make a comfortable living.

His boss had suggested he spend more time in Hilo because that branch needed a little extra guidance. Although Mark liked the Big Island, he hated being away from home more than a week at a time. He'd suggested bringing Betty with him, but he'd been told the Honolulu branch didn't need to be without an operations manager for that long.

Then there was the issue of Betty's anger toward

him this morning. What had he done to cause it? Betty wasn't the type to fly off the handle without due cause, so he had to have said or done something pretty bad. He rubbed his chin and mentally rehashed everything they'd said before the meeting, but everything had seemed perfectly fine until the last report had been read and the meeting was dismissed.

Mark forced himself to do all the necessary work that couldn't wait until tomorrow before the bank closed. Then he headed over to Betty's office, where her door was still closed. He could see the light streaming from beneath the door, so he knew she was still in there. He knocked.

There was a brief pause before he heard, "Come in."

He turned the knob, slowly opened the door, then stuck his head in. "Sure it's all right? You're not too busy?"

Betty was rubbing her temples. "It's okay. What do you need, Mark?"

"I came to offer you a ride home."

She thought for a couple seconds then shook her head. "I still have a few things to finish here. I can walk."

Mark wasn't about to get into an argument with her, so he just mumbled a few things then left. He wasn't sure what he said, so he knew it probably didn't make any sense, but he was confused.

Time to hit the waves—the best stress reliever in the world. Days like this drove men to do much worse things, Mark knew. The second he got home, he ran inside, changed, then came back out and grabbed the closest board. He walked the short distance to the beach.

"Wanna go for a walk?" Deanne asked the second Betty walked through the door.

Shaking her head, Betty replied, "No, not today." She didn't want to risk seeing Mark like they had so many times, but she didn't tell Deanne that.

"We can take a different route," Deanne said as she stared at Betty.

"Give me a few minutes to rest, okay?"

"Fine. I need to call Steve, anyway. He had me working the morning shift, and last I heard, his afternoon person had to go home early. Maybe he needs me to close the stand for him."

As Betty changed clothes, she could hear the low murmur of Deanne's voice while talking on the phone. Steve was such a sweet guy who'd made it big doing something he loved. That was what Betty was hoping for, too. Banking was something she thoroughly enjoyed, and she had her sights set on moving up as high as she possibly could yet still stay in Hawaii.

When she came out of her room, Deanne was grabbing her keys. "I'm gonna go help Steve close the stand. Wanna come with me?"

"No, you go ahead," Betty replied, thankful for the break. She needed to be alone.

"I'll only be an hour or two."

"Take your time. If Steve wants to go somewhere

afterwards, don't feel like you have to come back early for me."

Deanne laughed. "Okay, I can take a hint. You want to be alone. We can talk later."

That was one of the many things Betty loved about her roommate. Deanne wasn't one to get her feelings hurt when she needed to be alone. She didn't expect too much from their friendship, which drew Betty closer to her.

A half hour after Deanne left, the phone rang. She froze for a split second, wondering how she should react if it was Mark.

Finally, she grabbed the phone. "Hey, sis, it's me."

"Jeff!" Betty's heart raced at the sound of her brother's voice. "It's about time you got home." Then she remembered the party. "Are you home?"

"No, not yet," he said, laughing. "I just wanted to let you know the details of our arrival."

Betty scribbled notes while he talked. "I don't have a car yet, but I'm looking for one."

"Hey, don't worry about it. Lani and I can get a taxi. I just want to see you and hear all about your new job at the bank here. Is it any different working in Hawaii?"

"You know it is. How's Lani?"

His voice grew very soft. "Lani's wonderful, Betty. She makes me happy just by being in the same room with me."

Betty was beyond happy for her brother and dear friend. She couldn't have thought of a better match for either of them, although in the beginning she wasn't sure. Jeff had always been a ladies' man, and Leilani didn't have much experience in the romance department. However, her calm nature had relaxed Jeff, and they'd fit together like they were made for each other.

After Jeff gave her all the information she needed and told her how he couldn't wait to see her, they hung up. Betty smiled. Once Jeff and Lani were back, things would be much better.

Each time Betty heard a car, she jumped. After looking out the window a half dozen times, she realized she was being silly and overreacting. Besides, Mark wasn't likely to come here. He'd had a busy life before she arrived, and she was probably the furthest thing from his mind.

She grabbed the book she'd been trying to read for the past several days, but she still couldn't get into the story. Maybe doing a little housework would work off some of the anxious energy, so she got up and grabbed the broom.

The sound of the car door slamming caused her heart to hammer. She turned around just in time to see Deanne run through the door.

"Have fun?" she asked before she realized Deanne's face was devoid of color. "What's wrong?"

"There's been an accident," Deanne said slowly, shock registering on her face.

"What?" Betty leaned the broom against the wall. "Who?"

Deanne gulped. "Mark. Steve went with him in the ambulance. I have the van."

"What happened?"

"Come on," Deanne said. "Let's go. I'll tell you on the way to the hospital."

Chapter Eleven

"He what?" Betty said, not believing what Deanne had just told her.

Speaking very slowly this time, Deanne repeated what she'd already said. "Mark wasn't paying attention to what he was doing, and he slammed into the breaker wall."

She sat in the passenger seat, staring at Deanne in disbelief. This couldn't be happening. Mark wasn't a fool. Plus, he was too good of a surfer to have done that. "That's insane. What was he thinking?"

"We don't know. He was unconscious when the lifeguard pulled him out of the water."

"Where were you and Steve?"

"We were getting ready to leave. Steve had me handle the customers returning their boards while he balanced the daily receipts. All the commotion in the water got our attention, but we figured it must have been a tourist who didn't know what he was doing. We were shocked to find out it was Mark."

Betty felt sick inside. As angry as she'd been at Mark, she never wanted anything to happen to him.

"I wonder what he was doing," Betty said barely loud enough for Deanne to hear.

"Who knows? Steve said Mark's had a lot on his mind lately. Is he having some kind of problem at work?"

"No," Betty said slowly as she thought back to earlier in the day. "Quite the opposite. He's one of the most respected managers there."

"You do know Steve offered him a partnership, right?"

Betty didn't answer. Instead, she asked her own question. "Do you think he'll take it?" After a few seconds of silence, she added, "That is, if he's all right?"

Deanne shook her head. "Don't say that. Of course he'll be all right. Mark's a healthy man. We gotta think positive."

"Yes, of course."

They rode the rest of the way to the hospital in silence. Betty felt chills running up and down her spine as thoughts of Mark's injuries raced through her mind. What if he was paralyzed? Or worse, what if he didn't pull through?

"Okay, hop out," Deanne said as she pulled up in

front of the emergency room lobby. "You go on inside and I'll find a parking place."

Betty did as she was told. As the double doors opened, she stepped into the tiled lobby and looked around. Steve was sitting in the corner, holding onto a can of soda, hunched over his knees, staring at the floor. He looked like he'd been through the wringer.

"Steve," Betty said as she approached.

When he quickly glanced up, Betty saw the drawn look in his eyes. She'd never seen Steve like this. It must be serious.

"They don't know anything yet," Steve said, his voice hoarse. "But it doesn't look good."

Betty's knees nearly gave out, so she sat down next to him, reached out, and gently rubbed his back. Deanne walked in a few minutes later and sat on the other side of Steve.

Every few minutes, either Deanne or Betty stood up to check on Mark's status, and the nurse at the desk said he was still in surgery. Finally, nearly three hours after they'd brought Mark in, a doctor came to the door and looked into the lobby. Steve jumped up and quickly made his way over. Betty and Deanne were right behind him.

"He's out of surgery for now. His condition is stable but guarded. There's been some swelling to the brain, but it appears temporary. We won't know for about twenty-four hours. Why don't you go on home and get some rest?"

Betty shook her head. "I can't leave."

"Neither can I," Steve announced.

The doctor looked at all three of them. "Any of you related to him?"

"No," Betty replied. Then she realized someone needed to contact his family. "I work with him, and I have access to personnel records. Want me to call his family?"

"Yes," the doctor replied. "Have them call me here at the hospital."

Betty turned to Deanne. "Would you mind running me over to the bank?"

"Sure. Got your key?"

Patting her purse, Betty nodded. "I always keep it right here."

It didn't take Betty long to find what she was looking for. Once she had his parents' phone number, she asked Deanne to take her home so she could make the call. Deanne nodded.

A woman answered the phone. "My name is Betty Sorenson, and I work with Mark Diaz. Is this his mother?"

The woman said she was. Betty told her briefly what had happened and explained what she knew about his condition. Then she gave her the hospital phone number and hung up.

"That's one of the most difficult things I've ever done in my life," she said.

"You handled the situation very well," Deanne told her. "I would have stumbled over the words. How do you tell a parent their child is in serious condition?"

Betty raised her eyebrow and shook her head. "Mark isn't exactly a child. He's a grown man living on his own, working in a responsible position at one of the best banks in the country."

"True."

Mrs. Diaz's shaky voice played back in Betty's mind. "But you're right. He's still their child."

"Wanna go back to the hospital now?" Deanne asked.

"Sure, let's go."

By the time they returned, not only had Mark's parents contacted the doctor, Steve had spoken to them as well. "They're coming over on the next flight out of Los Angeles."

"Mark's from LA?" Betty asked. "I always thought he was Hawaiian."

"His parents have moved all over the world," Steve explained. "His dad's CEO of a major corporation that has offices everywhere."

"Oh," Betty replied, now realizing how little she really knew about Mark. "Have you met them?"

"No," Steve said. "But Mark's told me all about them." He grimaced.

"What?" Deanne said, nudging him. "I can tell you're keeping something from us, Steve."

"Mark's relationship with his father is very strained. I gathered, talking to Mark, that he had something to prove to his parents, which was what was holding him back from what I proposed." Steve glanced at Betty and stopped talking.

Deanne softly said, "That's all right, Steve. She knows."

Steve added, "As long as Mark stays in banking, his parents will stay off his back. I guess they consider that to be a respectable profession, unlike the surfboard business."

Betty and Deanne exchanged an understanding glance.

The next several hours went by in a haze. It was nearly daybreak when Betty and Deanne went back home. Steve told Deanne not to worry about reporting in for her shift. He said he'd find someone else.

Betty decided to take a quick shower and head into the office. "Are you nuts?" Deanne shrieked. "You haven't had a wink of sleep all night. How can you expect to work?"

"I won't be able to," Betty admitted. "But people in the office need to know what's going on. I'll be home in a couple hours."

Shaking her head, Deanne trudged toward the bedroom. "Don't expect me to wait up for you. I'm gonna go catch some Z's, and I don't expect to be up until sometime tomorrow, unless we hear something about Mark."

Betty didn't even feel tired. She knew why. She was too revved from worry and the stress of what had happened to Mark. If she'd been able to see him, she might be able to relax a little, but the doctor only allowed Steve into the room—and that was only because Steve had accompanied him to the hospital.

She begged the doctor to let her in, but he shook his head, saying he was only following hospital policy. "What if he wakes up?" Betty asked.

"When his parents arrive, we'll see," the doctor said.

Betty's frustration grew with every moment. She was tired but knew she wouldn't be able to sleep any time soon. As she showered and dressed for the office, she rehearsed how she'd let people know of Mark's accident.

The first place she went was to human resources. Andrea saw her right away.

"What can I do for you, Betty?" she asked, grinning. "Still love your job?"

Betty licked her lips and nodded. "Yes, of course, but that's not why I'm here." As she told Andrea about Mark's accident and condition, silence filled the room.

"This is terrible," Andrea said as she tapped her pencil. "On top of being a great guy, Mark is such an asset to the bank, and he'll be missed on the job. I hope he fully recovers. Any idea of the prognosis?"

Shaking her head, Betty told her she still didn't have any idea yet and that his parents were flying in as soon as they could. Andrea told Betty to go on home and get some rest, saying she'd take care of letting everyone else know.

"Thanks," Betty said. "I'll talk to Mark's supervisor and secretary, and you can tell the rest. If I hear anything else, I'll let you know."

She turned to leave, but she ran smack dab into

Fran. "Hey there, Betty!" Fran said. "I was worried about you when I arrived and you weren't in your office. I thought maybe you'd been in an accident or something."

Betty started to tell her about Mark, but she hadn't said anything to Mark's secretary yet, and she didn't want Fran's big mouth to be the initial source of information about Mark's condition. "Give me just a few minutes, Fran," she said. "I need to talk to a couple of people, then I have something to tell you."

Fran tilted her head to one side, frowned, then nodded. "Okay, I'll be at my desk after I talk to Andrea."

Betty spoke to Mark's boss and secretary, then headed straight for Fran, who was shaking her head, tears streaming down her face. "This is so awful, Betty," Fran told her. "Mark's too young to be a quadriplegic."

Did Fran know something Betty didn't know? "Where did you hear that?" Betty asked, her heart falling to her feet.

"Andrea told me about the accident. It's terrible. There was a guy back in high school who had a surfing accident, and he'll never walk again. To this day, he's still riding in a motorized wheelchair, without the use of his arms or the ability to walk."

Betty breathed out a sigh of relief. She was also glad she hadn't told Fran about the accident first because of her overreaction. "Don't jump to conclusions, Fran. We don't know what the prognosis is."

Still shaking her head, the same grim expression etched on her face, Fran replied, "It can't be good."

Betty had to get out of there or she knew she'd say something she'd later regret. "I'm going back to the hospital, Fran. If anyone needs me, I'll have my cell phone on."

"Okay. If Mark wakes up, tell him we're thinking about him. And tell him I know of a great support group where he can learn to cope with his disability."

Instead of arguing, Betty said, "Fine. See you later, Fran."

The woman was about to drive her crazy. Betty walked outside and angled her face toward the sun. The humid, salty air felt good on her skin, and the fragrance that wafted from the nearby plumeria tree gave her a warm, familiar feeling all over. She picked a couple of the flowers to take to Mark, just in case the doctor relented and let her in to see him.

Steve was waiting for her when she arrived. "Mark's parents will be here in a couple hours," he said. "I told the doctor to ask if you could go in to see him, and they said they didn't see why not."

Bless Steve. Betty turned and offered him a smile of gratitude. "Can you go with me?"

"Sure," he said as he escorted her to the nurses' station.

The nurse on duty led them to Mark's room. "Don't be alarmed at all the equipment and tubes," she said. "He's doing quite well, and we expect to be able to take him off the respirator soon."

Steve raised his eyebrows. "That's great news." He turned toward Mark, who lay there, his eyes closed, his face handsome as ever. "Hey, Mark, Betty's here."

At first, Betty thought Mark's flinch was her imagination, but Steve pointed and smiled. She reached out and gently touched his hand. It moved.

"I think he remembers you," Steve said. "That's a very good sign."

Betty had to control the shakiness of her voice as she softly told Mark about the flowers she was placing on his table beside his bed. "When you wake up, at least you'll have a piece of the outdoors."

They were able to stay in Mark's room for about ten minutes, before the doctor walked in. "We have to turn him now. Why don't you go on back to the waiting room for a while?"

Steve guided Betty back to the area with the teal vinyl chairs. "Want some coffee? I can go down and get us both some."

She nodded and stood. "Sounds good, but I want to go with you. I don't want to sit here too long, or I'll start imagining all sorts of bad things."

They went to the hospital cafeteria, got two cups of strong coffee, and sat down at a table beneath the very bright fluorescent lights. "All hospital cafeterias are exactly alike, whether you're in Arizona or Hawaii."

Steve chuckled. "I've never been in a hospital cafeteria until now."

"You're kidding."

"Nope. Everyone I know is pretty healthy." He

slammed his hand on the table. "Man, I sure hope Mark gets better. He's too young for something like this to get him down."

"Come on, Steve. I've known you for years. It's not like you to be pessimistic."

His eyes were misted over when she looked directly at him. "Mark's a great guy."

"Yes," she agreed. "He is definitely a great guy."

There was a moment of uncomfortable silence before Steve spoke again. "So, how do you like your job here in Hawaii? Is it the same as back in Arizona?"

Since it was obvious Steve wanted to change the subject, Betty decided to go along. "Some things are almost identical, but I like working here better."

"Deanne says you love banking."

"Yes, I love it."

"Would you like to move up with this bank?"

Betty snickered. "Of course. I'd like to be in charge of all Hawaiian branches one of these days."

"I have no doubt that'll happen," Steve said. "You're a very smart lady."

"Thanks, Steve," Betty said as she reached out and patted his arm. "You're a sweet guy."

"Hey," he argued, "don't tell anyone else that. You'll ruin my reputation."

"Deanne doesn't have much school left," Betty reminded Steve as she made small talk to kill time. "What is it? One semester?"

Steve's expression changed the moment Betty mentioned Deanne's name. "Yeah, one semester. She told me she needs to concentrate on her studies until she's finished, so I guess that means I won't see much of her."

"She'll still work for you, won't she?" Betty asked.

"Only to fill in when people call in sick."

Betty could tell this wasn't a good time to have this discussion with Steve. It was obvious that he and Deanne had agreed to back off, and he didn't want to talk about it.

They sat in the hospital cafeteria for almost an hour before Steve glanced at the clock on the wall. "We better get back, just in case Mark wakes up and asks for someone."

Betty jumped to her feet and led the way. She was as eager as Steve to see how Mark was doing.

"Anything new?" Steve asked the nurse when they returned.

"No, not yet. He's still holding his own, and we think everything will be okay."

Steve thrust his hands in his pockets and walked back over to Betty. She'd heard the nurse, so he didn't have to repeat it.

They took turns pacing and asking about Mark. Minutes and then hours passed. Betty was beginning to fade rather quickly, and she wasn't sure how much longer she'd be able to stay awake.

Then a sound of people arguing came from the door. "We're going to get our son back home where he belongs. I told you we should have made him stay there."

"We can't make Mark do anything. He's a grown

man." The woman's voice was very soft. "He likes it here."

"I just didn't offer him the right incentive," the man said in a very authoritative tone.

Was that Mark's parents? Betty looked at the attractive couple standing inside the emergency room lobby, appearing to be in a state of shock over this whole thing.

Steve jumped up and crossed the room before she had a chance to react. She remained seated as she heard him introduce himself.

"I want to see my son," the woman said, turning her back on Steve and marching toward the double doors leading to the rooms.

The nurse stopped her. "We're almost ready to take you back there. The respiratory therapist is with him now."

Betty remembered the flower she'd brought. She jumped up and got the nurse's attention, telling her she hadn't been thinking when she'd brought the flower into his room. "I hope I didn't cause a problem."

The nurse smiled. "No, we saw it and thought it was very sweet, but we took it out, just in case."

Mark's mother pointed her finger toward Betty and glared at Steve. "Who's she?"

Betty started to answer for him, but he spoke up quickly. "She works for Mark."

"Oh." The woman turned her back to Betty, while Mark's dad moved toward the nurse.

A few minutes later, the nurse told them to follow her, and she'd take them to Mark. The second they were gone, Steve said, "Those are the rudest people I think I've ever met. I can't imagine having parents like that."

Betty had been thinking the exact same thing when Mr. and Mrs. Diaz came back out. They hadn't been back in Mark's room more than a couple of minutes, and they were already causing a commotion.

"He simply can't stay here. What kind of hospital is this?" Mr. Diaz said.

"This is an excellent hospital," Steve said, defending the place.

"I'm going to make arrangements right away to have him moved to LA, where we can keep an eye on our son."

Betty's heart fell. Mark had no say in this matter because he was still unconscious. She bit her lip and didn't say a word, while Steve stood next to her, seething, she could tell.

Since Mark's parents were at the hospital, and Betty hadn't slept all night, she accepted Steve's ride home. As she got out, Steve thanked her for being such a good sport.

"What do you mean?" she asked.

"You roll with the punches. You never get rattled. I can see why Mark has confidence in you." He paused before adding, "He cares a great deal about you, too."

"Did he say that?" Betty asked.

Steve grinned. "Don't tell him I told you, okay?"

"It's our little secret." She slammed the van door shut and ran inside.

The house was quiet, Deanne was still sleeping. As carefully as she could, she changed into a very loose-fitting T-shirt and boxer shorts and crawled beneath the covers. Her body was screaming out for sleep, she was so tired.

Both Betty and Deanne were awakened by the sound of the telephone. As Betty sat up, she wondered what time it was.

"Are you gonna get that?" Deanne groaned from her bed.

She grabbed the phone off the nightstand which was between the twin beds. It was Steve.

"Mark's awake," he said without even telling her who he was.

"He's awake?" Betty repeated loud enough for Deanne to hear.

Deanne sat up in bed and mouthed for Betty to tell her what was going on. Betty nodded as she repeated everything Steve told her.

"How can they do that?" Deanne asked when Betty got off the phone and told her about Mark's parents making arrangements to take him back to the mainland with them.

With a shrug, Betty said, "I have no idea why they'd even want to, with him in such bad shape. He's been in a coma for almost a whole day, and they're ready to fly him over the ocean? I don't know what they're thinking."

"Sounds selfish to me," Deanne said.

Betty had been thinking the same thing, but she didn't want to say such awful things about people she'd barely met. "I hope they ask Mark what he wants. That's what's important."

"If he leaves Hawaii," Deanne said slowly, "I'm afraid he may never come back."

A cold feeling washed over Betty as she realized how important it was for her to talk to Mark. "Let's get dressed and go see him, okay?"

They arrived at the hospital an hour later. Steve was in the lobby, waiting for them. His face was drawn, his eyes were bloodshot, and he looked like someone had kicked him around. But still, he stood up and smiled at Deanne.

"Feeling a little better?" he asked.

Deanne nodded. "Yeah, but what's going on with Mark?"

Slowly, Steve shook his head. "The doctor's in there right now, talking to Mark and trying to make a decision. From what I understand, Mark does not want to leave and the doctor wants to keep him here, but his parents are talking to their lawyers."

"Can they do this to him?" Betty asked. "He's a grown man, and if he's not in the coma anymore, can't he make his own decisions?"

"I think they're using his head injuries to say he's incompetent."

"Oh, that's ridiculous," Deanne said. "When can we talk to Mark?"

"As soon as the doctor's finished with him, but before his parents get back. They've given strict orders to not let anyone in to see him." Steve paused. "But the doctor thinks letting us in will help him get better."

Several minutes later, the doctor came to the door. "Mark was asking if you ladies were here yet. Wanna come on back?"

All three of them followed the doctor down the hall. Betty held her breath, trying to brace herself for what she might see. To her surprise, Mark was sitting up in bed, smiling, even though she could tell he was in pain from his pinched expression.

"Hey, man, how's the head?" Steve asked.

"We're thinkin' that board might have knocked some sense into me," Mark said quickly, letting everyone know he was sharp as ever. "I'm gonna have to deal with a giant headache for a few weeks." He grimaced. "I hurt in a few other places I don't want to mention, too."

"Take two aspirin and call me in the morning," Steve joked.

"I'll do that." Mark turned to Deanne and smiled. "Not much longer before you're back in school, is it?"

"Only a couple weeks. I'll be glad when it's all over. I'm sick of school." Deanne turned to Betty and winked then grinned back at Mark. "You're looking good for someone who got beat up by your surfboard."

"Thanks a lot." Mark smiled but held his head very still. Betty could tell he was in extremely intense pain, but he didn't want to complain. Then he carefully cut his eyes to Betty. "How's the bank? Getting along without me?"

"It's only been for a day," Betty replied. "Everyone at the office sends you their best."

With a smile, he held her gaze for a few seconds before saying, "Yes, they did, didn't they?"

Betty felt all her blood rush to her face.

"Thanks, Mark."

"It's true." Mark shifted as he looked over at Steve. "Have you heard what's going on with my parents?"

They all nodded. "Anything we can do to keep you here?" Steve asked.

"I just signed some papers, and the doctor has declared me completely competent and able to make my own decisions."

"That's good," Steve said. Betty wondered if he believed Mark would be able to stand up to his parents' lawyers, which no doubt were probably the most expensive and the best money could buy.

"When I get outta here, I'll be making several decisions," Mark continued. "This accident was a blessing in disguise. I wasn't kidding when I said that surfboard knocked some sense into me."

Steve reached out and touched Mark's shoulder as the sound of Mark's parents' voices came up the hall. "We'll be seein' you later, man. Don't get into too much trouble."

"That'll be hard, but I'll do my best."

Betty swallowed hard. "Bye, Mark. Call me if you want anything."

Mark tilted his head forward, then grimaced. He wasn't kidding about that headache. "I'll call you in a few hours."

As they left, Betty realized they were in for a long battle. Mark's parents had smug looks of determination on their faces, and she had a feeling they wouldn't stop until they got what they wanted.

Chapter Twelve

"Mark, you'll get the best of care back home," his father told him. "These people are not equipped to deal with the kind of head trauma you've endured."

"Dad, I already told you, I'll be fine. This hospital handles surfing related accidents all the time. The doctor has told me I'm not likely to suffer any long-term damage." Mark's head ached too much to argue, but he had to stand his ground.

"How would he know? Has he run any tests? Where's all the latest high tech equipment?" He glanced around as if trying to prove his point.

Mark let out a sigh. These people were the most stubborn and strong-willed people he'd ever known. And they were his parents. He loved them, but he had a different outlook and way of doing things.

"I'm staying right here," Mark said.

Mark's mom glanced at his dad with one of those looks like they'd expected this. "Mark, honey, you really need to listen to your father. I'm sure you're worried the bank won't be able to get along without you, but we have to think about your health."

"And your future," his father added.

Mark was fully aware of how important his career was to his parents. After all, he had his father's image to live up to.

He'd had a few hours of lying here in this bed, thinking about what he really wanted out of life, and it wasn't hard to figure out. That blow to the head showed him how quickly things could change and how valuable life was. He wasn't about to let life get away from him without at least trying something he really wanted to do. It was time for him to act and quit dreaming.

"Like I said, Mom, I'm not leaving."

"We've spoken to our attorneys, son," his father said.

"I figured you would. I guess I'll have to spend my entire savings hiring my own attorneys. You might break my bank account, but you're not breaking me."

Mark knew he held a tone of defiance that his mother claimed he'd had since he was a toddler. But he meant every last word of it, and he refused to back down.

"You're forcing us to do something we'd rather not do."

Mark tried to shrug, but his shoulders ached. Instead, he set his jaw. "You'll do what you feel is best, but I'm not changing my mind."

"Is there a girl?" Mark's mother asked.

"Maybe."

He didn't think it was his imagination that his mother flinched as she looked at his dad. She tugged at his arm and said, "Come on, let's leave for a little while so Mark can rest."

As soon as they were gone, he let out a deep sigh. As impossible as his parents were, he knew they loved him in their own way. All of his childhood was spent in the care of a nanny, and he often longed for the warmth of being held in their arms. But his father wanted him to grow up strong and independent, and he figured the best way was to not coddle Mark. And there were times when he wasn't sure his mother agreed with the way he was raised, but she never defied her husband.

Mark *was* strong and independent, but not in the way his parents wanted. He was determined now more than ever to live his own life without worrying about what his parents thought. His distraction was what had caused the accident in the first place.

"I wonder what's going to happen next," Deanne said as Steve pulled into the driveway at the castle.

"Mark's a smart guy. He'll figure out a way to do what he needs to do." Betty could tell there was a note of sadness between her friends. Maybe one of these days, after Deanne finished school, she'd have more time to nurture a relationship with Steve. Funny how Deanne had always been the one who seemed boy crazy. And now that she was so close to having something real and lasting, she was the one who'd put the skids on. Betty respected Deanne's decision to hold off furthering anything with Steve.

"Powerful attorneys are hard to fight," Betty told them. "I'd hate to see Mark beaten down by attorneys just so his parents can get their way." She'd heard about his parents from Steve, but until she'd actually seen them, she hadn't realized how hard it must have been for Mark to leave them. Her respect for him as a man went up several notches. It also explained some of his mannerisms in the office when she'd thought he was a sourpuss. He had a lot of baggage.

"I think we should go back to the hospital in a little while," Steve said, "if for no other reason but emotional support. Mark needs it right now."

Deanne agreed. "Are you coming with us, Betty?"

"Yes, of course."

The phone rang, and Deanne answered it. Holding it out, she smiled and said, "It's for you, Betty."

"Hey, sis, we're back."

"You're early!"

"Yeah, well, Lani was starting to get homesick, and I had a few things I needed to take care of, so we cut the trip short."

"That's great, Jeff."

"Wanna get together and celebrate?" he asked.

Betty suddenly remembered the surprise homecoming party they'd planned, but at the moment she didn't feel like celebrating. She briefly gave him an overview of what was going on. Jeff was sympathetic and made all the right sounds. "Want me to come over?"

She started to tell him it wasn't necessary, but she really missed her brother, so she said, "Yes, that would be nice. Bring Lani."

"I wouldn't go anywhere without her." Then they hung up.

Still smiling, Deanne said, "Jeff's coming?"

A stricken look covered Steve's face. "You used to go out with him, didn't you?"

"That was a long time ago, Steve. Besides, he's married now."

That didn't seem to change the panic in Steve. Betty had to force herself not to smile, but she knew it would only add insult to injury. She looked away.

Jeff and Leilani were at the castle in fifteen minutes. After hugs all around, Lani took a step back and shook her head. "Nothing's changed in this place."

Betty laughed. "Of course it hasn't. We don't want to tamper with perfection."

"So what's the deal with your boss, Betty?" Jeff asked, abruptly changing the subject. "You say his folks are forcing him home?"

Betty and Steve explained all the details, letting Jeff know as much as they knew. He nodded and asked questions.

"What's this guy's last name?"

"Diaz," Betty and Steve said in unison.

Jeff's eyebrows shot up. "Diaz? His dad's name wouldn't be Manny Diaz, would it?"

Betty had no idea, but Steve frowned for a moment then nodded. "Yeah, I think that's the name. I heard him say that when he answered his cell phone."

Jeff chuckled. "The guy's a shark, but I know how to deal with him."

"You know Mark's dad?" Betty asked.

"He's been wanting me to take over the training in his computer department for nearly a year, but I've been playing the negotiation game with him."

"You're kidding," Deanne said. "It's a small world."

"I've bid on nearly every large business in this country, so I know a few people."

Betty figured there were very few important business people her brother didn't know. He'd never been a shy person.

"I know a few of his hot buttons," Jeff added. "But first, I'd like to meet the guy who has my sister's heart."

"I never said—" Betty began before Jeff cut her off.

"You didn't have to say a word. I know you, Betty. Your eyes light up when you say his name."

Betty looked to Lani for help. But she didn't get any. Lani only nodded and said, "Jeff's right. Your eyes totally sparkle."

"That's probably just lack of sleep," Betty said, trying to save herself.

Everyone laughed. Deanne piped up, "Oh, sure." Then they laughed even louder.

"Wanna go meet Mark?" Steve finally asked Jeff.

"Sure, let's go."

Lani tugged at Jeff's arm. "Do you think it's such a good idea for all of us to converge on the guy while he's lying in a hospital bed? Why don't you and Steve go, then we can follow in a little while. After you come out, Betty can see him."

Jeff looked lovingly down at his new bride. "As usual, you're right."

Deanne let out an audible sigh. Jeff was still smitten with Leilani, and Betty figured that would never change. She was the sweetest person Betty had ever known, yet she also had a quiet strength.

Steve handed Deanne the keys to his van, and he left with Jeff. "Give us about an hour," Jeff instructed.

"Yes, sir," Betty replied. Her brother could be so bossy at times, but now, she appreciated it. This was one of those times she was too emotional to make rational decisions.

"While we're waiting, tell me all about your job here," Lani said.

Betty was thankful for the mental distraction, which she knew Lani had done on purpose. She told Lani everything she could think of, from how Mark had tried to put her on a beginner's training program, to how he'd called for her to help him with Nancy in the Hilo office.

Lani grinned. "This thing with Mark is a really big deal, isn't it?"

"You can say that again," Deanne said. "That's all she ever thinks about."

This time, the sigh came from Lani. Betty saw her two closest friends exchange a knowing glance, and her face grew very hot. She could no longer deny her feelings for Mark. In the beginning, she kept telling herself he was such a grouch, there was no way she could fall in love with him. But now that she knew him better and saw what he was like outside of work, her feelings were too intense to hide. She was deeply in love with the man.

After the guys had been gone an hour, Deanne grabbed the van keys and said, "Let's go."

Without another word, Betty and Leilani followed her out the door, into the van, and they were on their way. "I don't need to go into his room," Lani said. "He doesn't know me, and I don't want him to be uncomfortable. I'll just wait in the lobby."

When they arrived, Betty was surprised to see her brother standing outside the hospital talking to Mark's father, who was nodding and looking very agreeable. That puzzled her. Last time she'd seen Mr. Diaz, he was frowning even more than Mark had when she'd called him a sourpuss.

"Hey," Jeff said as they walked up. "C'mere and meet my newest client."

"This is your sister?" Mr. Diaz said, pointing to Betty.

"The only one I've got," Jeff said as he pulled Betty close to him on one side and Lani to his other side. "And my wife Leilani. Aren't they wonderful?"

Mr. Diaz coughed. "Uh, yes, I s'pose."

Lani stuck out her hand and smiled at the man she'd just met. "I'm so pleased to meet you, Mr. Diaz. I'm sure you'll be more than satisfied with my husband's work. He's the best in the business."

"Yes, I'm well aware of that." Suddenly, Mr. Diaz appeared very distracted as he turned back to Jeff. "Are you sure this hospital can handle my son's injuries? I have access to the best medical care in the States."

"This *is* one of the states," Jeff reminded him. "And yes, he'll be well taken care of here. His doctor is the best I know of in head trauma. They deal with many surfing accidents, and they know exactly what to watch for."

There was some hesitation as Mrs. Diaz joined her husband. They exchanged a quick glance before she turned to Jeff. "Are you sure?" she asked. Concern for her son was evident in her voice and pained expression.

Jeff nodded with conviction. Betty was impressed as she watched her brother convince these two stubborn people that their son needed to stay right where he was. Finally, Mrs. Diaz nodded.

"It's probably not a good idea to move him," Jeff said, driving his point home. "The long flight would probably set him back quite a bit in his recovery."

Mr. Diaz sighed. "In that case, I guess it would be better to leave him right where he is."

Betty shouldn't have been surprised. She'd seen her brother work magic on many people, all her life. Jeff had a way of winning people over and gaining their trust, and he never let them down. Too bad he had to take a client before he was ready, but she sure did appreciate it.

"Why don't we all go in and see Mark?" Deanne said. Betty glanced over at her and saw that she was already backing toward the hospital entrance. "Oh, Jeff, where's Steve?"

"He's with Mark right now. Mark asked his dad and me to leave so he could talk business."

Betty quickly turned toward Mr. Diaz, thinking that would upset him, but he appeared unfazed. Apparently, talking business was okay, regardless of his son's condition. She didn't understand that at all.

"I think I'll go on back to the hotel now," Mr. Diaz said. "My wife's not feeling well. The time difference and jet lag are difficult on her." Not to mention her emotional state, Betty thought.

As soon as Mr. and Mrs. Diaz had left, Betty grabbed Jeff's arm. "I really appreciate what you did for Mark."

"I didn't do a thing," Jeff said.

"You took his father's company on as a client for Mark, right?"

Jeff shrugged. "I was going to sooner or later anyway. I figured I might as well go ahead, considering the circumstances."

When Betty glanced over at Lani, she saw how proud Lani was of Jeff. They made a beautiful couple, both in looks and in spirit. These two were made for each other.

The nurse stopped them before they got to the double doors. "You may all go in there, but you can't stay long. Mark needs his rest. He's been through a lot."

Steve was sitting in the chair by Mark's bed, and they were talking in very low tones. Mark lifted a hand and waved, causing Steve to turn around. He stood up.

"Ready to make your announcement, partner?" Steve asked Mark.

"Sure, might as well." Mark sought out Betty and looked her directly in the eye as he said, "I've decided to get out of banking and go into business with Steve."

Betty let out a gasp. She thought he might decide to do something with Steve, but she hadn't expected him to quit the bank.

Steve belted out a laugh. "Don't act so shocked."

Mark motioned for Betty to get a little closer. "I'm losing my voice," he said hoarsely. "But before it's completely gone, I wanted to let you know I think you'd be perfect for my old job. I even called the regional director, and he seems to think that's a good idea. That is, if you want it."

Betty didn't know what to say. She just stared at Mark.

"And I was kind of hoping we could pick up where we left off before you got mad and dumped me."

"I never got mad at you," Betty said. "And I certainly never dumped you."

Mark glanced over at Steve and rolled his eyes before he looked back at Betty. "Okay, if you say so. I don't want to argue with such a smart woman."

Deanne groaned. "It's not that he doesn't want to, Betty, it's just that he knows he can't win if he does."

Everyone laughed.

"Oh, one more thing," Mark whispered, causing Betty to lean over so she could hear him better. "After I'm up and able to walk down an aisle, will you marry me?"

Betty's knees almost gave out beneath her. Steve was quick, though, and he stuck a chair behind her, which she found with Deanne's guiding arm. She first looked at Mark, who was smiling, then she turned and looked around at everyone staring at her. They all knew. She'd been set up. But then common sense got ahold of her.

"Uh, Mark, how can you ask me something like that at a time like this?" She glanced nervously over her shoulder before turning back to face him. "Besides, we haven't exactly had a normal dating relationship."

Mark chuckled. "Look, Betty, I've been a businessman for a while, and I've seen all kinds of mergers. I know when something's right."

Folding her arms over her chest, she squinted and said, "I don't know. Do you think my new job will give me enough time for a relationship? It does involve some travel, you know."

Mark reached out and took her hand in his. "I just happen to love traveling, especially when it's with the woman I love."

"In that case, I guess that might be a good idea." She reached down and gently brushed her lips over Mark's. While she was still close enough for only him to hear, she said, "This time it was okay to set me up, but you'd better not ever do it again."

"Yes, dear," he said. "Anything you say, dear."

Jeff chuckled. "You're treading on dangerous ground with my sister when you make an offer like that. She'll never let you forget it."

"And I wouldn't want her to," Mark said softly as he smiled back at Betty.

She suddenly thought of something. "How about your parents?"

Jeff lifted a finger. "We already discussed this with Mark's dad." Betty saw Mark and Jeff exchange a glance before he turned back to face her. "He seemed a little uneasy at first, but Mark convinced him—with Jeff's help, of course. He's okay with it."

"Am I the last to know about this?" Betty said, amazed at how everything had happened.

"Apparently so," said a voice from the door. Betty turned around and saw Mrs. Diaz. "In fact, I just got off the phone with your mother. She's nearly as delighted as I am."

"Delighted?" Betty said, not believing the complete about-face in attitude.

"Oh, yes," Mrs. Diaz said as she smiled at her son. "Anyone who makes my son sit up in bed with a headache like he must have must be pretty special."

"She's more than special, Mom," Mark said.

"Just make sure you don't try to do too much too fast," Mrs. Diaz warned, her voice cracking. Betty now knew Mark's mother was genuinely concerned for Mark, and her own heart softened toward her.

"Mom, we'll be just fine."

With a tear in her eye, Mrs. Diaz nodded and offered a slight smile. "I'm sure you will."

Betty let out a sigh. She'd always been the competent one—the person who'd organized things and made sure everything had been taken care of. Obviously, she'd met her match in Mark Diaz.